I0536389

KILLER POINTE

KRISTI HELVIG

Dark
Edge
Publishing

Copyright © 2020 by Kristi Helvig

All rights reserved.

No part of this book may be reproduced in any form or by any electronic or mechanical means, including information storage and retrieval systems, without written permission from the author, except for the use of brief quotations in a book review.

Cover Design by The Cover Collection

ALSO BY KRISTI HELVIG

The Wing Collector

Wingless: The Wing Collector Short Story Prequel

The Missing

The Boy Who Wasn't There

Countdown Cafe

Burn Out (re-releasing Summer 2020)

Strange Skies: Burn Out Book 2 (re-releasing Summer 2020)

For the dancers of the world
Dance on

1

———

I stared straight ahead, my left hand on the barre. The strains of music washed over me for the tenth time in a row. My right arm arched overhead, my toe pointed as it slid over the polished floor. The whole studio reeked of sweat—whoever thought ballet was girly had never smelled the tail end of a three-hour session.

Adrian moved throughout us, picking up an arm here, clucking disapproval there, encouraging "more focus" everywhere. He stopped next to me and I sensed his eyes studying my form.

"Nice, Bree" was all he said before he moved on to Catelyn. "Chin up, Catelyn," I heard a second later, and I swear the heat of her glare penetrated the back of my head. Like she needed another reason to hate me.

Adrian strode to the front of the class and stopped the music. "Enough. What I'm seeing today is causing me physical pain." His crisp, slightly-accented voice sounded harsher than usual. "If classical music could be damaged by inept ballet, Tchaikovsky's work would be bleeding up here. Do you hear me? Bleeding." He clapped his hands. "Go home. Practice. Do better."

I sighed and picked up my bag, my feet aching from the pointe shoes. As the others girls filed towards the door, Catelyn threw me a dirty look over her shoulder.

"Don't forget," Adrian called, and all heads swiveled toward him. "Sleeping Beauty auditions are one day away. That's tomorrow, for the math challenged among you. It will be in addition to the regular practice days this week. Practice, people."

Like I needed to be told that. Even when I wasn't in class, I was dancing—at home, in the grocery store aisle while Mom picked out chicken cutlets, even during passing period at school when no one was looking. Ballet was fun for me, the same way that catching a football was fun for my little brother. I'd practice until my feet cracked and bled, and then I'd bandage them up and practice some more. No wonder Adrian seemed to like me—I didn't mind torture.

In the hall, I tried to change my shoes as quickly as possible without drawing any attention, but I heard the whispers.

"Bree, the magnificent, will play the part of Aurora," Catelyn said, in an exaggerated imitation of Adrian's voice. "In fact, we will be changing the title of the play from Sleeping Beauty to Sleeping Bree."

Several girls snickered. I wanted to stand up and yell that the ballet had nothing to do with the real story of Sleeping Beauty anyway—that I had actually been there when it all went down, but that would get me locked up in a psych ward which would make getting to the audition problematic.

"Knock it off, Catelyn, you're just jealous," Ava said while yanking a wayward bobby pin from her hair. I looked up and smiled at her. It's not like I left a lot of time for friends, but Ava was one of my closest. "Bree can't help how intense Adrian is."

Another girl chimed in, "Yeah, it's like he thinks he's leading the New York City Ballet instead of a group of kids from the 'burbs."

Relieved to have the focus off of me, I pulled my jacket on and zipped it all the way up. I couldn't risk catching a cold before the audition. Maybe the other girls weren't as intense about dance as me, but ballet was in my blood and Julliard was in my future. Or so I hoped. The money issue was a problem, but if things worked out right, my unusual side job would take care of that.

I pushed past the throng of girls and stepped outside. The chilled night air blasted my face. Geez, you'd never know it was only October. I shoved my hands into my pockets, looking for the keys to my car. Having my own car was supposedly one of the perks of being a "good girl," according to my mom.

Never mind all the minuses, like staying far away from parties or having the cutest guy in class look straight through you as though you didn't exist. I braced myself against the wind and hurried toward the vehicle my mom called "Old Reliable." I just called it old.

"Bree-ee, wait up!" Ava had a way of drawing out my name the same way my little brother did.

I whipped my head around. "Hey, A, thanks for sticking up for me in there."

She hurried to my side. "Don't listen to Catelyn. She can be sort of a bee-atch."

"Sort of?" I asked.

Ava smiled. "She can't help it. She feels threatened by you."

I grinned at her. "No wonder I like you so much."

She shuffled her feet back and forth. "Also...I wondered if I could catch a ride home with you." Her breath formed icy rings in the air.

She'd never asked for a ride before, but I hadn't seen her mom's car around in awhile. "Yeah, sure."

Ava beamed at me and hoisted her bag over her shoulder. "Great. Thanks. My dad's at soccer practice with my brother, and my mom had to work late again."

"It's not a big deal," I said, though actually it was a pretty big deal because the fact that we were friends didn't make me any less mortified to have her ride in my junker car. I had to get in the driver's side door and lean over to pull up the lock on the passenger's side.

"Sorry," I said. "I'm pretty sure this is the only car left in circulation without automatic locks. Don't tell everyone how lame it is."

Ava pulled the door shut while I cranked up the heat. Strange noises churned from inside as the heater engaged. "No problem. At least with its color, you'll never lose it in a parking lot."

I cringed. That had been my dad's exact wording when he'd

painted the car neon green. Getting a great deal on this piece of crap car had been a source of pride for him.

"Who needs fancy shmancy bells and whistles?" he'd told me while tinkering under the hood. "You just need something dependable to get you from Point A to Point B." He'd "surprised" me with the color one weekend after I'd been away at ballet camp.

"I guarantee you, B, no one will have a car exactly like this one," he'd said, patting the car on its blindingly green hood. He couldn't have been more right about that.

I didn't have the heart to tell him that because of my car, some kids at school had taken to calling me Kermit. Most of them drove new Audi's or BMW's. I knew of one kid who drove a used BMW, but even that was only a year old—his mom had decided she wanted a different color and then gave him her old one. My car was one year, plus a few decades old.

I didn't realize I'd been silent until Ava spoke again. "I didn't mean that in a bad way. I mean, it's great you have a car to drive. My parents won't buy me one ... well, another one. It was just one little accident, and it was barely my fault, you know?"

Even though that meant it was totally her fault, I nodded. Flaunting my perfect driving record wouldn't win any brownie points. I turned onto Main Street and headed toward our subdivision.

"About the play," she said in a rush, "I know you're going to get the lead ... you totally deserve it, but do you think I have a shot against Catelyn for the Lilac Fairy?"

I didn't want to crush her spirits, but Catelyn was really good. Not at all disciplined, and she obviously spent more time on her nails than her pirouettes, but she had talent. Ava worked harder than anyone in class, well, except for me, but she always struggled with the moves. It just didn't come as naturally for her.

"Sure, A, you've got a great chance," I lied.

Ava heaved a sigh of relief. "Whew, thanks for the vote of confidence. I'm gonna practice as soon as I get home, well, after my stupid algebra homework. You're so lucky you're in A.P. and don't have to deal with Ms. Lerner. Did you know she has no eyebrows? She draws them in. I heard it's because she has trich ... trich..."

"Trichotillomania?" I offered as I turned onto a side street.

"Yeah, that. It's weird, huh? Anyway, you're so awesome for taking me home. Oh, I almost forgot, we're gonna hang at Trevor's house party next weekend, right? I haven't gotten my groove on in a while. I think Rae is going with us too. I need to call her and double check."

"Uh, no, I don't think so," I said, pulling up to her house. Though I'd never been hesitant to perform classical dance on a stage in front of hundreds of people, the thought of jamming to bands I'd never heard in a room full of classmates made me downright queasy.

Ava patted my shoulder. "It'll be fun. You know Ty Wilder will be there, but rumor is that he's officially going out with that fake-nailed, fake-haired, spray-tanned she-devil. Anyway, we don't need guys, we've got girl power."

It figured. The hottest boy in school—the one who had never noticed me despite having several classes together—had been lured by the carefully cultivated appearance of Catelyn Grey.

I tried to smile. "Maybe. I'll think about it." Watching Ty and Catelyn grind on the dance floor was the least fun thing I could think of.

Ava opened the car door. "Yay! I'm taking that as a 'yes.' Okay, see you tomorrow, and thanks again." She hopped out and waved several more times on the way to her front door.

I breathed deeply as I pulled away. My only prospects for dance partners were my friends. Go me.

It wasn't that I was shy—but aside from my little circle of friends, I didn't fit in with any particular crowd. Ballet wasn't exactly a contact sport, so I didn't fit in with the jocks. I was smart but wanted no part of the extra-curricular clubs that the nerds geeked out over, so they didn't understand me. I'd hoped to fit in with other dancers, but no one at my studio seemed to take dance quite as seriously as I did. My dreams involved seeing my name up in lights at Lincoln Center.

MOM WAS RACING around the house when I got home, her cell phone in one hand and a protein bar in the other. The faint smell of canned tomato sauce lingered in the air.

"Thank goodness you're home," she said, and planted a kiss on my head. "My shift starts in half an hour. Cal is finishing up his homework and then he needs to get to bed." She yelled into the other room. "Hear that, young man? Don't give your sister any trouble."

"Got it, Mom," his little voice called back.

Mom wore her scrubs with the rainbows and unicorns all over them. She had an assortment of scrubs featuring various flowers, zoo animals and cartoon characters. Since she worked as a pediatric nurse on the oncology floor of the local hospital, she said it was important for the kids to see her as someone "fun." That they needed a little something to brighten their day.

Working the overnight shift brought in more money, and since Dad died, we never seemed to have enough. His death seemed to make her even more determined to keep her patients from dying. Maybe part of it was guilt that his heart attack happened while she was at the hospital saving other people, and no one was there to save him. Well, I was there, but I couldn't save him. I tried. In the end, I could only hold his bluish-colored body while tears streamed down my face as I waited for the ambulance.

Mom gestured to a plate on the counter. "Leftover pasta for you. Reheat for one minute and pour some sauce on it...it'll taste good as new." She kissed me quickly again. "Have a great day at school tomorrow. Hope dance class went well."

"It was great. Bye, Mom." And she was gone. She wouldn't be home until after my brother and I left for school the next morning. She slept during the day, but always tried to be up by the time we got home. On ballet days—which was most days—I barely got to see her.

I dumped the plate of pasta down the garbage disposal and grabbed a Diet Coke and some Fritos. I carried my loot into the family room, rumpled Cal's dark hair, and slumped into a chair. "What's up, kiddo?"

He grinned, displaying the hole where his tooth had been the day before. "Lost another tooth. The tooth fairy's gotta pay up tonight."

Shoot. I'd have to scrounge through my clothes to find a couple bucks to stick under his pillow. He was only six, the age I'd been when Mom adopted me, so I didn't have the heart to bust the whole tooth fairy myth yet. He'd been an unexpected surprise when I was ten, years after Mom was told she couldn't get pregnant. "Awesome, Cal. What are you savin' up for?"

He didn't hesitate. "The new Madden game. It's so cool. I can make my own fantasy team and have real play-offs and go to the Super Bowl and everything."

I smiled. "Dude, you lost me at Madden."

Cal jumped up and headed towards his Nerf football. "C'mon, Bree. Throw me a few passes before bed. I'll finish my homework in the morning."

I shook my head. "No can do. Mom would kill me. Tell you what —after school tomorrow, I'll take you to the park and we'll run drills."

His eyes lit up. "Promise?"

My heart heaved. Going to the park to play catch was something he did with Dad every weekend. Now that Dad was gone, I knew I should step up more to do the "boy" stuff he loved so much. There weren't enough hours in the day to be a sister, daughter, student, dancer, and dad.

"I promise," I said, and crossed my heart. "Now let's get that homework finished and get you to bed."

AFTER HE BRUSHED HIS TEETH, Cal lugged out the heavy book of fairy-tales that Aunt Laura had given him. I'd protested at the time but she'd insisted that the swords and dragons made the stories as fun for boys as for girls and told me that I should be more "open." I couldn't reveal my real problem with the book so I kept my mouth shut.

I sighed and gestured toward his football-shaped clock on the dresser. "It's a little late. Maybe we should pick a shorter book."

"No, puh-lease," he whined. "George and the Dragon won't take that long." He settled on the bed and looked at me with such hope that I couldn't say no.

I read the story in my best brave knight voice and tried not to roll my eyes. I wondered what Cal would say if I told him that George was really a whiny, snot-nosed wimp and that I was the one who had killed the dragon. Cal probably would have laughed and asked me to "make up" another story. I had to hand it to her Royal Highness—she had some good PR people.

I PEEKED in Cal's room a little past midnight and his face looked angelic in the glow of his Star Wars nightlight. Sleep wasn't something that came easily to me, especially on the nights Mom worked. There was also this irrational part of me that worried something could happen to Cal on my watch—like he could die on me the same way Dad did. Even on the nights Mom was home, I compulsively checked on him while he slept to make sure he was breathing. Sometimes, I'd crawl into his bed and sleep awhile, like the power of my presence could keep harm away.

Satisfied that he was dreaming of end zone dances, I slipped a five-dollar bill under his pillow. It was all I could find, so I'd let him think the tooth fairy had upped her payment rates. I scribbled a note with a pen filled with iridescent ink—it seemed like something a fairy would have. After putting the note next to the money, I went back down the hall to my room.

I'd be dead at school tomorrow if I didn't get some sleep, so I pulled on my favorite cotton pajama pants dotted with tiny dancers doing arabesques and pulled on my headphones. I scrolled to the score of Swan Lake and hit play. The intense, enchanting melody filled my head and I tried to relax. My eyes started to close when something shimmered in the dark.

I bolted upright, yanked the headphones off my head, and stared into the shadows of the room. There it was again. A faint sparkle and shifting of the air.

No. This was too soon. Cal needed me. My heartbeat sped up and thudded beneath my breastbone.

The airflow increased, spun faster, and whirled into a sparkling black funnel.

Fueled by frustration, I tried to resist. I gripped my bedpost with my hands, but felt my body being pulled across the room. It was useless—there was nothing I could do.

I let go.

2

She was prettier than me. They all were. She laid very still, her long golden hair fanned out over the satin pillowcase. I crept closer. Her skin shone like flawless ivory; her lips pink as roses. I hoped I wasn't too late. No, there it was, the slight rise and fall of her chest. She was alive.

A slight breeze stirred the clouds and a sliver of moonlight escaped, lighting up part of the tower room through the window. I glanced outside. The tiny opening led to such an expansive, yet unreachable view. How sad.

I headed back down one flight of stairs. The scent of rain clung to the air and dampness permeated the stones in the wall. A lantern would give me away, so I used my hands for guidance. My feet were nimble, and I grazed one of the slick stones with my shoulder. It couldn't be much farther.

I reached the landing and hesitated. My heart raced like it always did when I got to this part. I moved down the hallway and guessed this particular door would be locked. It was.

I reached in my pocket and pulled out my trusty lock-picker. A nice perk of the shifting was that I always landed here with my work gear, aka, a sword and small pick attached to my traditional tunic and leggings. After fiddling with the lock a minute, I was rewarded with a click. I put my ear to the door and turned the knob. It opened with a slight creak and I froze but relaxed at the sound of heavy snoring. This one didn't feel the need for guards like some of the others. I leapt to her bedside and in one smooth movement, unsheathed my jeweled sword.

Her white hair stuck out in curls around her head and wrinkles sunk deep into her face. A smile played at her lips, as though she dreamed of sweets and puppies. She almost looked like someone's kind, if somewhat eccentric, grandmother. Almost.

I plunged the sword deep into the woman's chest. Her eyes flew open and she gasped once, her gnarled hands clawing at the weapon. I pushed the sword in deeper and her hands fell to her sides, her eyes still open but no longer seeing.

After placing coins on her eyelids, I wiped my sword clean and raced down the remaining stairs, out into the night. The cloud cover had dissipated, and stars twinkled in the brisk air. I ran back toward the forest where the Queen's horse waited for me but glanced back at the tower room.

"Don't worry, princess," I whispered. "Your prince will come."

THE AIR SMELLED of dew and flowers as I galloped across the meadow toward the Royal Village. A crescent moon glowed in the clearing sky. If Majestic, the Queen's steed, could keep up her pace, I'd reach her kingdom in a few hours. I'd be back to my world, and Cal, very soon.

The time passed differently here—days equaled mere hours in my world, which worked out well after Dad died. Before, if I was summoned in the middle of the night, I knew Cal would be fine even if Mom was working, because Dad was there. Now, it wasn't so simple. It killed me to leave my brother even for a few minutes. But a contract was a contract.

Several heavily armed guards escorted me through the corridor that led to Her Highness. Ornate tapestries woven with gold thread hung from the walls. The marbled floors were beautiful but cold under my slippers. The guards didn't speak. They never spoke to me. We stopped at the heavy, gold-leafed doors that led to her private chamber. Before the guard could knock, the door flew open.

I bowed my head, trying to contain my smile, then gave up and grinned at him. "Hello, Rolph."

Rolph didn't even acknowledge the guards. He winked at me and grabbed my arm, pulling me inside and shutting the door in their faces.

He kissed both my cheeks. "Bree, darling, it's so good to see you."

"You too." I linked my arm through his as we walked through a small chamber toward another door. Without a doubt, Rolph was my favorite person in Liralelle. Over the years, I'd told him all about my life in Philly, while he shared his ultimate desire to quit the Queen's service and set up a boutique in the Center Village. He also believed in true love and was on a never-ending quest to find it. "So, what's new, Rolph? How are things with the stable boy?"

He rolled his eyes. "Edward? He turned out to be more bark than bite if you know what I mean, and I much prefer the bite."

I laughed. "Of course. But you deserve to be happy—I want you to find someone special."

Rolph sighed and looked serious for a moment. "Me too, darling. Me too."

We reached the door, and he fished a key from his pocket. "She's in a mood today," he whispered, fingering the edge of his lavender scarf. "Think it was a spat with the King. He left for another 'hunting excursion.'"

I covered my mouth to keep from laughing. Everyone knew the King's hunting excursions involved neither buck nor beast, but rather buxom women who had a thing for chunky men in power.

"Seriously, Bree. Watch yourself," he warned.

Rolph opened another door and we entered Her Highness's private area. She was alone, save for a waiting maid and a skinny, pimply-faced man-boy. Her copper hair lay in perfect coils atop her head, and her diamond-encrusted gown sparkled. The soft lighting in the room cast shadows which minimized the appearance of the wrinkles around her eyes. If one looked at her quickly, she might even seem young.

Rolph led me to her throne, then stood off to the side. The ceremonial incense sent wafts of fragrant herbs up my nostrils. My nose twitched as I tried to contain a sneeze.

I bowed low, sweeping to the floor. "Your Highness."

She waved her hand impatiently. "Is it done?"

"Yes, it is done."

The pimply-faced boy spoke in a squeaky voice. "The witch is really dead?"

"Yes," I answered.

He clapped with glee. "Then Rapunzel is mine to claim?"

I sighed. "She's all yours."

"Wait," the Queen said. "We need to follow protocol. Rolph, bring in the treasurer and recorder."

Rolph bowed and left the room, leaving me with the timid chambermaid, the Queen and the boy.

"Stand straight, Bree, so I may look at you," the Queen commanded.

I stood, suddenly aware of my long, tangled hair that needed washing and probably looked more black than brown. My shift was tattered and torn at the bottom, but it wasn't like I made my living serving tea to royalty.

Her Highness looked me up and down and made a sound that could only be interpreted as disapproval. "At least I don't have to worry about my husband with you," she said finally.

Rolph sashayed into the room, followed by a short, squat man I called Roly, but was really named Rologard, and Beatrice, a tall, wiry woman carrying a velvet-covered parchment book.

"Rologard, do you have the required payment for Bree?" the Queen asked.

He bowed. "Yes, your Highness." Roly turned to me and held out a small velvet pouch. "100 gold coins. Unless your rate has changed?"

I grasped the sack eagerly. "Nope. This was an easy one." I turned to the scrawny man-boy. "You might even have been able to handle it."

"That's enough," the Queen chided. "Beatrice, please read the oath."

Beatrice cleared her throat like she had the most important job in the world. "Bree, beast hunter of Liralelle, do you swear that by accepting the payment of 100 gold coins, you agree to the Eternal Records being changed?" She peered at me like I'd never heard this before and might change my mind. "Meaning that you will not exist on paper anywhere. All of the Tales of Liralelle, referred to as 'Fairy Tales' in your world, will reflect our new version of what happened tonight."

I raised my right hand, trying not to roll my eyes. We'd done this a hundred times already. "I swear."

She continued, "And do you agree that the Tales will state that the Princess, in this case Rapunzel, was rescued by her Prince," she turned to eyeball the pimply-faced boy, and did roll her eyes, "in this case, Prince Hubert?"

I fingered the riches in my hand and smiled. "I agree."

Beatrice marched over and handed me the elaborate book along with an ink-tipped quill. "Sign here," she ordered.

I signed *Bree* with a flourish and Beatrice solemnly handed the book to the Queen. Her Highness stamped the entry with a wax seal to make it official.

"May the record books reflect the agreed upon description of events," the Queen said.

Beatrice kissed the Queen's hand. "I will go and write the account immediately, your Highness. When do you want this Tale to appear in her world?" She tipped her head in my direction.

The Queen tapped her chin. "Hmmm ... a little over two-hundred years ago should suffice."

Beatrice nodded and left the room with Roly. The whole time-thing here amazed me. She could send the Tales back in time, so people reading them now in my world would think they'd been that way forever. I shifted my weight from one foot to the other, wanting to get on with it.

Prince Hubert stood, looking like a dog waiting for a bone. The Queen paused a minute before throwing it. "Go to her, Hubert. Tell her that you killed the witch and saved her. She'll love you forever."

"Better hurry, she'll be waking soon," I couldn't help adding.

Hubert bowed repeatedly to the Queen, walking backwards toward the door. "Thank you, your Highness. Thank you." He sprinted out the door as soon as Rolph opened it.

I noticed he hadn't thanked me once, even though I was the one who had made it all possible.

It was already like I didn't exist.

3

"Mom said you have to eat something before school. How 'bout a banana?" I begged.

My little brother's eyes gleamed. "How 'bout a bowl of cocoa puffs?"

Our usual morning battle had begun, but I was more tired than usual thanks to my moonlighting. "Cal, your brain needs growth food, not crap food." I sighed. "Eat the banana and then you can have some ADHD in a bowl."

He grinned. "Deal."

I packed his lunch and backpack as I watched him attack his cereal. He would never understand how much I loved him, how much I wanted to protect him.

~

WITHIN MINUTES of arriving at school, Ava accosted me in the hall. "So, are you ready? I can't believe it's today. I'm so nervous. You're not worried at all, are you?" She didn't wait for an answer and bounced along next to me as we walked, her hands waving wildly. "You shouldn't be—you'll do great. I so hope I get the Lilac Fairy part—I mean, she is the most important fairy of all of them. Anyway, can I catch a ride with you to the audition? It would be fun to talk about strategy on the way there."

Rae's voice piped up from behind us. "Do you two ever talk about anything but dancing? Ballet is bad for you. I read that eighty-three percent of ballerinas have eating disorders."

Ava squealed and threw her arms around her. "Silly, Rae, you know we don't have eating disorders."

Rae hugged her back. "I know, which means most of the rest of your dance class does ... statistically speaking." She winked and stood back, her auburn curls falling over her shoulder. "S'up, B."

I grinned at her. Her mom was a shrink, so while most girls read Teen Vogue or Glamour, she read things like The Journal of Eating Disorders. Her dark purple nails complemented her hair and peace sign t-shirt. "We're gonna dance this weekend, right girls? I mean real dancing, not tutu stuff. No offense."

"We are so there," Ava said. "I need some fun in my life right now."

Ava was always so bubbly and excited that her response confused me. I opened my mouth to ask her what was wrong when, out of the corner of my eye, I spotted Ty Wilder several lockers away. Even while getting books out of his locker, he projected confidence and self-assurance.

"That is one beautiful human being," Rae said, following my stare. "Hey Ava, you need to make your move on him this weekend. I heard he and Catelyn are getting cozy, so you need to stop that action."

It sucked having the same crush as your best friend. I wanted to agree that he was beautiful but thought I'd give myself away. The bell rang.

Ava sighed. "Yeah, one day, when I grow some nerves. Gotta get to homeroom. See ya' at lunch." She and Rae made it halfway down the hall, before Ava turned and yelled. "Don't forget me later, I'll meet you by Kermit."

I cringed. She hadn't meant anything by it, but Ty had to have heard her. I peeked over at him and the smile plastered across his face. Anger sparked in me. My car wasn't that pathetic. Then I noticed the reason for his goofy smile. Catelyn stood on the other side of him, her hand tucked into his back pocket. Guess the rumors were true, but the fact remained that back pocket hand-diving was so lame.

I grabbed my books and slammed my locker. At least I had advanced classes with him and wouldn't have to see her until the audition.

"Hey, Bree. Are you ready for today?"

I swiveled my head in mock surprise. "Oh, hi Catelyn. I didn't see you there." Her hand was still wedged in Ty's jeans. "Yeah, I am ready."

Her fake smile seemed creepy, but maybe that was just me. She used her free hand to toss her blond curls over her shoulder. "I hope so, because I plan on challenging you for the lead. And I think I've got a good shot, if I say so myself." Her hot pink manicured nails sliced the air as she gestured with her hand. "You better watch out."

I stared from her to Ty, whose smile had vanished. He looked a little uncomfortable with the whole encounter.

What I wanted to tell her was that I killed trolls and hunted witches before she even took her appetite suppressants each morning. She was the one who better watch out.

"Good luck, Catelyn," I said instead, and walked away. Aside from being afraid of something happening to Mom or Cal, the only other fear I had was my irrational fear of zippers. Catelyn didn't bother me no matter how hard she tried.

AP English had a hard time capturing my attention the way it usually did. Even Ty Wilder sitting right in front of me couldn't distract me from obsessing about the audition.

I closed my eyes, practicing each and every part of the ballet in my mind. I wanted to be perfect today. My pirouettes were flawless and the ease of my mental performance excited me. I even visualized the other girls sitting on the floor, watching in awe while they awaited their chance. As I made my final turn and faced the imagined mirror, eager to see the approval on Adrian's face, I did something unthinkable. I tripped. I gasped as I stumbled, ending my audition on the floor instead of on my toes.

My eyes flung open. Several kids, including Ty, had turned to stare, so my gasp must have been audible. I stared down at my desk, willing everyone to look away. The teacher continued lecturing and everyone went back to taking notes. Everyone except me, because now I couldn't concentrate to save my life. What had just happened? I'd never had a bad performance ever, imaginary or otherwise. Whatever it was, it couldn't be a good sign.

The class bell finally rang, and I gathered my books as quickly as possible. Ty looked at me and opened his mouth like he was going to say something. Heat burned my cheeks and I turned away. I dug through my backpack and pretended to look for something until he left the classroom. I sighed and carefully zipped up my bag, making sure my fingers were far away from the teeth. Other people had to have odd fears too, right? The classroom was quiet.

"That's a first," said a voice behind me. "Not the staring at Ty Wilder during class part, but it's the first time you've openly gasped at his hotness."

I whirled around to face Jay Asher. He was quiet like me—he'd certainly never spoken to me before. "I was not gasping at anyone's hotness. I—I—"

"Hey, no need to get defensive." He laughed. "Just making an observation. I'm Jay."

"I know. We're in like, four classes together. You're just not usually so chatty."

He laughed again, and it sounded melodic. I noticed the instrument case in his hand. Oh yeah, I'd heard something about him being first chair of some variety. Some kind of prodigy band geek. I didn't know a trombone from a saxophone, though I knew it definitely wasn't a guitar case.

"I just figured I'd officially introduce myself, since it sounds like we'll be working together and all." He shifted the case to his other hand and started toward the door.

I didn't want to take the bait but I had to know. "Wait up," I said, hurrying after him. "What are you talking about?"

Jay stopped and grinned, revealing perfectly straight, white teeth. I wanted to tell him he had nice teeth, but that would be weird. "Word on the street is you're getting the lead in Sleeping Beauty. I'm playing trumpet in the orchestra for the performance."

It was my turn to laugh. "I'm not sure what 'street' you're on where people are talking about band and ballet, but okay. I don't know about the lead for me, but congrats to you on the orchestra. I've never danced in a production this big before—you know, one with live music."

He nodded, his brown eyes serious. "Yeah, it'll be the biggest thing I've done too—figure it'll look good on my resume for Juilliard."

"No way." I stared at him. "*I* want to go to Juilliard."

"Cool," he said. The next class bell rang. "Well, good luck with your audition."

"Thanks," I said. "See you in Trig."

One class down, six more to go, plus lunch. While visualizing more practice sessions during the next few hours, my thoughts still wandered to Ty, but occasionally veered to Jay. I'd never noticed how his eyes matched his dark hair. He was kind of cute in a non-obvious way. Unlike Ty, who was cute in an All-American, very obvious way. Jay even waved from across the room in Trig, and I smiled back. My goal remained to make Ty notice me, but it'd be nice to have a guy friend. Someone I could talk to without feeling like an idiot. I couldn't even speak to Ty—I'd probably fall over or something.

The seconds crept by, dragging along at a rate that made me want to shake the clock. Ava caught me between classes. "Oh, my lord, can this day go by any slower? I mean, it's killing me. Is it killing you? I just want to get it over with, you know?"

My body twitched, aching to let out the moves I'd been practicing all day in my head. "I know. I think the clock is messing with me."

"Bree?"

Ava and I turned at the same time. Ty Wilder stood in front of me.

The only reason I knew I hadn't hallucinated my name was that he was looking straight at me.

"Yeah?" My voice came out in a tiny squeak, and I wanted to disappear into the floor.

"I, um," he said, and cleared his throat. He almost sounded nervous, which would be impossible. With his piercing blue eyes and blond, spiky hair, he had nothing to be nervous about. "I just wanted to say I'm sorry, you know, about Catelyn this morning. I hear you're a really good dancer and all, so she's probably just jealous or something. Don't worry about her."

Catelyn wouldn't have admitted I was a decent dancer, even if someone threatened to break off one of her Razzledazzle Berry polished nails. I looked up at him, and he smiled. I smiled back and willed my voice box to engage. "Thanks."

He tipped his head toward Ava. "Hey, Ava. See you guys around." As he walked off, I wondered if I'd magically entered a different parallel universe aside from Liralelle—one where cute boys knew I existed.

Ava bounced on her feet next to me. "Aren't you gonna ask who told him you were a good dancer—okay, I won't make you guess. Me. It was me."

"Why on earth would you do that?" I asked, mortified, though I couldn't tell her why I was upset, because Ava was the one who "officially" had a crush on him.

"I had to," Ava said. "I heard him talking to Jake Horner about how much Catelyn wanted the lead, so of course, I had to step in. I said you were by far the best dancer—that the only way Catelyn would get the lead is if you didn't show up. I can't believe he likes that shallow bee-atch."

That made two of us. "No accounting for taste I guess."

Ava walked almost as fast as she talked, and I raced to keep up. "What's cool is I was so pissed when I heard him talking about Catelyn wanting the lead, that I wasn't even nervous at all to talk to him. Guess I just have to pretend I'm mad from now on. He's got the most amazing eyes, don't you think? I mean, I know all you think about is ballet, but you have to have noticed his eyes."

"Yeah, they're blue," I said, hoping she'd drop it.

Ava sighed. "You're completely hopeless."

SILENCE FILLED THE BALLET STUDIO. Nobody spoke as they prepared for the auditions, aside from a few hushed "good-lucks." Several girls stretched on the floor or against the wall, while others went through basic turns to warm up. Catelyn had ear buds in and tapped her feet on the floor in time to whatever music she was listening to. She wouldn't meet anyone's eyes.

Adrian clapped his hands. "Good evening. I trust I will see better performances than I did yesterday." He reached for his clipboard and sat in a folding chair. You will all dance the same number and will go two at a time. As we have studied all the parts, you will be performing Carabosse et la Fee des Lilas. One of you will dance the part of the evil fairy, Carabosse, and the other will play the part of the Lilac Fairy who softens the blow of her evil spell in order to protect Princess Aurora."

Ava squealed in delight. She could probably do the dance of the Lilac Fairy in her sleep. I only hoped Adrian could see how perfect Catelyn would be for the part of Carabosse.

Adrian glanced down at his clipboard. I hoped I was first so I could get it over with. "First up," he announced, "are Ava and Catelyn."

Catelyn pulled out her ear buds, a smirk on her overly powdered and lipsticked face. You'd think she was about to take center stage on Broadway—but her neon pink lips would be more appropriate on the nearest street corner. Ava fidgeted as she took her place in front of everyone. She looked ready to explode, her nervous energy having nowhere to go for the moment. Adrian tapped his chin a moment, studying them. "Catelyn, you do the Lilac Fairy. Ava, you're Carabosse."

Ava's face fell and my heart sank. It didn't mean that she couldn't get the part she wanted, but she'd probably been hoping that if he saw her dance the part, he would realize she was the perfect Lilac Fairy. The music started and I crossed my fingers for Ava. She recovered some of her composure but started in a few seconds late. Being as theatrical as she was, she still did a convincing Carabosse, conveying spite and malice through her dancing before Catelyn took over.

Catelyn danced like I'd never seen her dance before. She gave it her all. Her form was almost perfect, her frosted blond hair pulled back in a tight bun. Knots formed in my stomach. Even if she only danced better than me for one night, this was the night that counted. With a performance like that, she could easily grab the lead. The piece ended and there was a moment of total silence.

Applause erupted until Adrian slapped his hand against the clipboard. "Save the applause for opening night, people." He turned to Ava and Catelyn. "I see you both have taken my advice on working harder. Catelyn, very nice. Ava, a little more work on timing but overall, good."

Coming from Adrian, his comment toward Ava constituted high praise, but disappointment was etched on her face. She didn't think it was good enough. She sank down next to me, still breathing hard, and put her head into her hands. "Ugh. Why did I have to be Carabosse?" she whispered.

I patted her shoulder. "Don't worry. You were great."

Adrian called up the next two dancers, then the next two, and the two after that. Catelyn's Lilac Fairy was far better than anyone else's of the night, and Ava's Carabosse took top honors in my opinion—even with the timing issues. I ended up being one of the last two to audition. Catelyn's icy stare followed me to the front, as though she could will me to fall with her gaze. The other dancer, a shy girl named Sarah, shook her arms out.

Adrian eyed both of us. "Bree, you do Lilac. Sarah, try Carabosse."

Great. Now there was no way I could avoid comparison with Catelyn's performance. It was down to the two of us for the lead. I took a deep breath and closed my eyes. I just had to do it the way I'd practiced a million times before.

The music started. I waited for Sarah's part to lead into mine. My body moved in perfect synchronization with the melody. Muscle memory took over and the dance penetrated every pore of my being. The other dancers disappeared, even Adrian vanished from my awareness, and it was just me and Tchaikovsky. The sound of my shoes on the floor was all that registered as I whirled around the room.

As the end of the number neared, I relaxed. I smiled as I turned toward the mirror—and caught sight of something I didn't expect. A troll. He bowed in mock salute in the mirror's reflection. My eyes flew toward the girls and Adrian. No one else seemed to notice anything. My toe skidded on the floor and I stumbled. Gasps filled the room as I fought to keep myself upright. I curled my toes and dug them into the floor like my life depended on it. Unlike my imagined nightmare in class, I succeeded in staying vertical. Though I didn't fall, it was a definite error.

The last note ended and my right arm hovered in the air, a forced smile on my face. I tried not to show my anger because no one would understand. The Queen and I had a deal. She only sent for me when it was night in my world, so that my life would have the least amount of disruption. Though she'd warned me that an extreme emergency would override the rules, I'd never once had Liralelle events intrude on my waking hours. Trolls creeping into mirrors couldn't be a good sign.

Ava's clapping broke through my reverie. "Yay, Bree," she yelled. "Great job, Sarah," she added a second later.

Adrian scribbled on his clipboard, a frown on his face. "Okay people, good work tonight. The results will be posted before tomorrow's practice. Thank you."

Everyone filed out into the lobby, excitement and nerves mixing together. Several girls patted me on the way out, which made me feel even worse. Catelyn sauntered straight through everyone, a triumphant smile on her face, and marched out the front door. The nice part of me wanted to tell her she did a good job. The not-so-nice part won and said nothing.

"Seriously, it wasn't that bad," Ava said after everyone left.

I sighed. "The fact that you just said that, means it was that bad."

Ava shook her head. "No, you could barely even notice. Besides, everyone knows you're the best dancer. Adrian would be crazy not to pick you. I just hope I don't end up as 'Adult Woman in Waltz.' Even if I'm not Lilac, I really want to be a fairy."

"You won't be a small part," I said. "In fact, I thought you made a great evil fairy myself."

Ava laughed, and we pushed through the doors. It's not like I could change anything now. Adrian would make his decision, and I'd have to live with it.

"Do you need a ride home?" I asked when she stuck close to my side. If I hurried, I'd still be able to get Cal to the park for some quality football time.

She nodded, uncharacteristically quiet for a minute. "Yeah," she finally said. "If it's not too much trouble. Things are kind of weird at home right now."

I waited for her to say something else but she didn't and I didn't want to press it. "It's never trouble for you. I'm just over there." Kermit was on the far side of the parking lot, but its green shine was visible even in the dark. Guess the color had its perks.

I knew something was really wrong when we drove for an entire minute in silence. I glanced over at Ava. "Do you want to talk about it?"

She shrugged. "No big deal. It's just that my dad's been gone more and more with his work. When he is home, he's all about my 'brother the athlete.' Guess ballet isn't that interesting to him."

Ava's mom had always been the one to come to our recitals and drive her to rehearsals. I couldn't avoid the question. "What about your mom?"

Ava turned toward the window. I barely heard her over the loud whine of my heater. "Let's just say that my mom isn't convinced Dad's absences are entirely work-related. I'm not either, to tell the truth."

"Wow, I had no idea. I'm so sorry." I turned onto her street, but the air under the streetlights looked strange. Almost glowing. No flipping way.

"But instead of confronting him, she's shut down completely. The only thing I've seen her interact with lately is a bottle of vodka. It's a good night if she doesn't pass out until after she burns the frozen pizza."

The glowing grew brighter and I made out the form of a small funnel in the dark, just past her house. This had to be a joke. I'd never been called before midnight—when I was safe in the confines of my bedroom. Her Highness understood the dangers of attracting publicity in this world.

"Thanks for all the words of support. Guess nothing shuts people up quicker than family problems." She crossed her arms and stared out her window.

"I, uh ..." The funnel grew and picked up speed. If Ava looked straight ahead there was no way she could miss it. Luckily, her house was on the right-hand side of the street.

I peeled into her driveway. "Sorry, A, I just feel sick all the sudden. Can we talk about this later? I really need to go."

"Seriously? Wow, some friend you are." Ava jumped out of the car and slammed the door. She ran up the walk to her front door without looking back. I wanted to call out to her, but if she turned around, she'd see the tower of wind coming straight at me.

I didn't even wait for her to get inside. I put the car in reverse and gunned the engine. Since outrunning the funnel wasn't possible, I took the only other option.

I drove right into it.

4

"Bree, darling, you must let me do your hair one of these days." Rolph held a lock of my hair between his fingers and rubbed it. He clucked his tongue in disapproval. "It's so dry. Some oil of hibiscus would do wonders for you."

I blinked while trying to wrap my brain around the fact that Kermit had made the trip to Liralelle. Plunked down against the backdrop of the majestic courtyard, it looked like an even bigger eyesore than in my world.

I brushed Rolph's hand away. "Why am I here again so soon? I'm supposed to be hanging out with my brother. You of all people know why that's so important to me. What's going on?"

He sighed, but his eyes traveled back to my wayward hair. "Her Highness needs you. There has been some trouble in the center Village." He looked like he wanted to say more but didn't.

I gaped at him. "What? I was just here and things were fine." My hand flew up to smooth my dark curls. "And stop staring at my hair."

Rolph chuckled and took me by the arm. His perfectly coiffed blond locks contrasted with the royal blue of his ruffled blouse. We headed to the Queen's chamber.

"Seriously, I can't stay long. My mom and Cal will freak out if I don't come home tonight."

His shiny shoes clicked on the polished floors. "Bree, you know time passes differently here. It's been months since you were last here, though it probably seemed like a few days in your world."

I snorted. "Try *one* day, as in yesterday."

"Look at the bright side," he said. "You'll be back home soon and your absence will have been mere minutes there." He winked. "Just tell your mom that you took the scenic route home."

Rolph reached the chamber door and opened it with a grand, sweeping gesture. "After you, madam."

A smile tugged at my mouth. No one could accuse him of lack of dramatic flair.

The Queen sat erect in her throne. It wasn't as ornate as her throne in the Great Hall, but it was pretty nice for a piece of bedroom furniture—way better than the IKEA chair in my room at home. She seemed oblivious to both the servant boy fanning her with a huge palm frond, and the maidservant rubbing oils into her feet. Her gaze focused out a window that led to nothing but the vast forests that surrounded her castle. Rolph stood off to the side, and I knew he hoped he wouldn't be excused—he loved him some gossip.

I bowed before her. "Your majesty."

Her attention turned my way. "Oh Bree, thank goodness you're here."

Like I had a choice. Although in truth, I did. I agreed to be her hired sword, chose to use my skills to defeat evil—knowing I could be called upon whenever necessary. "Rolph told me there has been some trouble since I was last here."

The Queen wiped her brow with a silk handkerchief. "Trouble like we've never seen before."

"I don't get it," I said. "Liralelle is a fairytale land—*the* fairytale land. Everything is supposed to be happy here, aside from a few bad guys." It was one of the reasons I liked the job—things were simple. My job was cut and dry, because Liralelle was black and white. Wasn't it?

Most of the people here were good guys, and when an evil person showed up, I took them out. Of course, I also loved the pay. I'd planned to use my earnings to fund my Juilliard tuition. At some point, I'd cash in the growing pile of gold coins tucked away in my bedroom to attend my dream school. I didn't get how people afforded school by working minimum wage jobs.

She sighed. "Things don't seem so happy here lately—there are even rumors of a revolt."

I shook my head. "That's awful, but what can I do about that? I'm a mercenary, not a revolution-queller."

The Queen put her hands in her lap and stared into my eyes. "That's what I'm telling you. Someone is behind this. Someone is stirring up my subjects with vicious lies and poisonous words."

Now that was more up my alley. "Do you have any leads?" I hoped she did, and I really hoped it wasn't a troll. Witches, warlocks, even fire-breathing dragons were easier to manage than the trolls. They had some kind of Napoleon complex that made them infuriating to deal with.

"It's a witch," she said, lowering her voice.

Rolph rolled forward on his feet, trying to catch everything she said without being noticed.

I stretched. "Perfect. Same rate?"

"No."

I arched an eyebrow at her. It was a shame that Liralelle was having troubles and all, but no way would I accept a pay cut. I opened my mouth, but she raised her hand to silence me before I started. "Your pay will be 10,000 gold coins. I believe that will be well worth your time."

Rolph let out an audible gasp. My mouth fell open. I tried to calculate the current price of gold in my world, but that amount should more than fund my entire time at Juilliard. "But why?"

"If this witch is who I think it is, she's more powerful than any enemy we've had in Liralelle. She's been quiet for years but must have been biding her time. She means to destroy everything I've created."

I frowned. I'd killed every enemy I'd been assigned since I contracted with Her Highness on my thirteenth birthday. In four years, I'd never once had an assigned target get away from me. A sickening realization washed over me and goose bumps broke out on my arms.

The only monster I'd never caught was the one whom I saw for an instant when I was six years old. It was the other reason I signed up for this job.

"You ... you mean this is *the* witch?"

The Queen leaned forward in her throne until her face was close to mine. "Yes, Bree, this is the one you've been training for all these years. I believe this is Muriel, the witch who killed your family."

old. Wet. That was all that registered. I opened my eyes and realized why—Rolph was splashing icy water on my face.

I tried to turn my head, and noted I was lying on a velvet couch in the sitting room. "Cut it out. I'm awake already."

Rolph pulled his hand away. "Sorry, but you fainted, my dear. I cannot believe all this. I'm so sorry. I remember when all that happened like it was yesterday."

My body felt numb and I tried to prop myself up on my elbows. Images flashed through my head and I tried to shut them out.

Coming home for dinner and finding them all dead on the floor around the hearth. My parents and my five-year-old brother. The old woman standing over them with her gnarled teeth and wiry hair. Her watery eyes fixing on me, as she motions toward me with a crooked finger. "Come here, dearie," she is saying. I run away into the woods.

I was six and defenseless—I never understood why she didn't kill me too. Once upon a time, my given name had been Kaia. After that, her Highness had used her powers to bring me to a parallel reality known as Earth, in order to keep me safe. She'd dropped me off in front of a church-run orphanage with a fake letter and vanished before they opened the door. I still don't know what the letter said, but the lady who opened the door hugged me after reading it, whispering, "You poor, poor dear." That was when I learned my name had been changed to Bree.

I stared up at Rolph. "Do you think it's really her?" I whispered.

He shrugged. "No one can disappear forever, and the Queen sure seems to think it's her. She's had her guards looking for Muriel for years ... let's just say that they have a lot of brawn but lack in the intellectual department." He lifted a steaming cup to my lips. "Now drink this tea. It'll perk you up."

The pungent, sweet liquid warmed my throat. "Thank you." I sat up on the couch.

Rolph's eyes held concern and something else.

"What is it?" I asked, reaching for his hand.

He took my hand and patted it. "It's just that ... the Queen is concerned you might not take the job. I've never wanted you to back away from a job before, but I don't have a great feeling about this one."

I attempted to smile. "Well, that's why I'm getting paid the big bucks, right?"

A frown line appeared between Rolph's eyebrows. "Sweetie, it'll be hard getting yourself to the Juilliard audition if you're dead."

"Guess I have to make sure I don't end up dead then." I sounded more confident than I felt. My insides turned to ice when I thought about the old woman. All I had to do was conjure up those memories and it was as though I were six again, instead of seventeen.

I stood up and gulped the rest of the tea. Rolph raised a single eyebrow. "And where do you think you're going?"

"For a ride in the woods. It always helps me to sort things out." I set the teacup on the settee and gave Rolph a quick hug.

"I'll have Edward ready Majestic for you. Be mindful of the goblins—I hear they've been in a foul mood lately." He rested his hand on my arm. "What should I tell the Queen?" he asked.

I patted his shoulder. "Tell her I'll give her my answer when I return."

FOREST SURROUNDED the castle on all sides. Once outside the wrought iron gates of the palace grounds, stone-paved paths curved toward different sections of the kingdom—each with its own village. Unless I had a job to do, I never ventured along the trail to the troll village—it would be the equivalent of pulling out your own toenail just for the fun of it. Trolls sucked. I passed by the branch-off with a crooked wooden sign stating "Troll Village", and breathed a sigh of relief when nary a troll could be seen. Even Majestic seemed to perk up when she realized we were heading a different way.

The trail narrowed as it reached the densest part of the forest. I patted Majestic as she treaded carefully through the foliage. We came to a fork in the road and breathed in the heady fragrance of flowers.

Though it was October back home, flowers here in Liralelle bloomed year- round. There were no seasons; the climate stayed mild and temperate aside from occasional rain showers. The big storms that came through were rare, and usually caused major destruction.

The road veering off to the left went by some goblin huts, Red's house, and Snow White's cabin, or "Snow Slut" as she was known in the goblin village. The trail to the right meandered through more forest, then cut through vast fields of flowers which surrounded a lake inhabited by fairies and water sprites, toward Cinderella's castle, where after several more miles, it ended at the Center Village.

I had no desire to mingle with a large group of people, and Her Highness ordered me to stay as far away from the villages as possible. It kept my identity protected—I was little more than a rumor among the villagers. A few who lived outside the village walls knew me but kept my secret.

The wildflowers in the fields called to me and I headed toward them, feeling a strong pull toward the main village despite orders. The trees started to thin and dappled sunlight lit up the landscape. A lilting voice could be heard ahead of me, and the sound of girlish singing filled the air. Her voice grew louder as she approached, and she rounded the bend with her basket swinging on her arm.

"Bree! Majestic!" she yelled, as she ran and threw her arms around the horse. "I missed you two."

"Hey, Red," I said, smiling. I jumped down and she gave me a fierce hug as well. "Aren't you a little far from home?"

She grinned and twirled around, her cape fanning behind her. "Nothing to worry about since you took out that wolf for me. Thanks for giving Old Mr. Coon the credit. He's the talk of the town." She looked around us and leaned closer to me. "And don't worry, I haven't told anyone about you." She pretended to lock her lips with an imaginary key.

"No problem." I tried to look stern. "But that doesn't mean there aren't other bad guys out there. I wouldn't wander too far from home for a bit."

Red wrinkled her nose at me. "Oh, that's why you're here, right? There's a bad guy in town?"

"More like a bad lady. Worse than the others." I patted her head. "Run home now."

Red cocked her head to one side, her pigtails swinging in the air. "Wait, are you talking about Muriel?"

I froze. My hands clenched into fists, and my chest tightened. All these years, I'd wanted nothing more than to find the witch responsible for killing my family. Every evil creature I'd killed along the way had helped to prepare me for her. I just hadn't counted on the fact that I'd be so scared. When I came face to face with her, I wasn't sure whether I'd use my sword efficiently like I did every other time, or if I would just break down and cry.

"What do you know?" I asked, incredulous that I was getting intel from a ten-year-old.

The little girl shrugged. "I've never seen her—just heard some folks whispering about her and her creepy eyes in the village. Something about 'Muriel's return.'" She made air quotes with her fingers. "Now your turn—tell me some more about your land of Philadelphia. It sounds so magical."

I shook my head at Red. "No time now, but trust me, the words 'magical' and 'Philadelphia' are rarely used in the same sentence. Anything else you heard?"

She shook her head. "No, but you should try the Center Village. Those old biddies are gossiping their heads off about it." Red whipped a checkered scarf off of her basket of bread. "Here, put this over your hair and you'll look more like a villager. Next time I see you, I'm not leaving until you tell me another story about your world. Got it? Good. Bye, Majestic." She skipped off into the forest without waiting for an answer, humming like she didn't have a care in the world. I couldn't imagine what that felt like.

Great. It looked like I'd have to go to socialize—not my strongest suit. My job involved killing evil-doers, not making small talk.

Majestic and I made it out of the trees, and I inhaled the sweet scent of flowers wafting across the fields. Shades of pink, yellow, blue, and purple that didn't exist in my world lay before me, sweet and spicy in their fragrance. Tiny fairies with shimmering, clear wings darted among the flowers. Though they were notoriously shy, a few approached to check me out before they zipped away again.

The bright blue water in the pond sparkled. Sprites flew high into the air before diving straight down and disappearing beneath the clear surface. A few children laughed and played tag in the tall grass, barely giving me a glance. The sunshine warmed my skin, with only a few puffy clouds drifting lazily across the sky. I wished I could stay longer but had to keep going. A movement in the tall grasses at the water's edge caught my attention. I pulled on Majestic's reins with one hand, while my other hand reached down toward the hilt of my sword.

"Who's there?" I called out.

A young woman stood up. Her dirty blond hair was pulled back in a loose ponytail and pond water sloshed inside the bucket in her hand. "Oh, hey, Bree. It's just me."

I relaxed. "Hey, Ella. What are you doing down here? Did your step-sisters give you the day off?"

She snorted. "Hardly. I needed a few minutes away from those wenches. Told 'em I'd fetch some water for their baths. I'm making it extra special for them." Ella made a hacking sound, and spit a big wad of snot into the water. "There. Think that's special enough?"

I laughed and tapped my sword. "You let me know if it gets too much for you."

Ella hoisted the bucket up over her shoulder. "Oh please, I can handle them. I'm fixin' to get the hell out of here soon, you know, takin' a little bit of gold here and there from the step-monster." She eyed me. "You're the one that might be needing help from what I hear. You need back-up to help with that crazy old biddy?" Ella flexed her arm muscle. "Because I've got a pretty good right hook."

Good news traveled fast. "I appreciate the offer, but I think I'll be okay. Take care."

Ella shrugged. "Suit yourself. You know where to find me if you change your mind." She stomped off toward their cottage. The thought of the step-sisters bathing in snot made me laugh again, but I wondered how much of her bravado covered up the loss of her mom. Red and Ella were the only ones outside of the Queen's castle who knew me well—sure, a few rumors floated now and again about a foreign warrior but no one knew for sure except those two. I'd offered Ella my services several times in the past—for free as the Queen hadn't ordered it—but Ella was a trooper. Hope she got away from the awful women who called themselves family.

I led Majestic to the water and let her drink, then continued the short distance to the village. As riding into town on Her Highness' horse would attract unwanted attention, I tied Majestic to a tree just outside the village and walked the rest of the way, making sure to cover my head with the scarf.

I'd always imagined the place would have a sleepy-town vibe involving maidens chatting while gathering water from the well, older women haggling with vendors over the price of fruit, and bored children chasing chickens through the street. If it ever had that vibe, it had disappeared.

Only a few things were as I envisioned. A cobblestone path, adorned with gas lamp streetlights, wound its way through the quaint shops along the main street. Hand-carved signs proclaiming everything from antique books to magic potions hung outside the stores. The stores themselves appeared to be open for business as usual. Everything else that might once have been described as sleepy, now looked more like panic.

Townsfolk gathered in small bunches on the street. Furtive whispers rose from each group, before one would race to others and pass along some tidbit. It was like an archaic game of telephone. The facts had likely long since merged with rampant rumors. A small girl with tattered clothes turned and stared at me. She tugged on the dress of the older woman next to her, and I ducked into the nearest doorway. I didn't want to hear superstitions; I wanted information. My best bet might be one of the shopkeepers.

I turned around and inspected the store, Ye Olde Magic Shoppe. Assorted candles, potions, and bottles lined the shelves while wands of all sizes and colors hung from the ceiling.

"Welcome," said a scratchy voice in the direction of the counter.

I peered across the store but couldn't see anyone.

"How can I help you, dearie?" She walked out from behind the counter. I hadn't seen her because she was shorter than the counter. A frizzy, white bun sat atop her wrinkled face. She wasn't a troll, or goblin, but was too short to be human—plus she looked about a thousand years old.

Her laugh came out gnarled but kind. "You're trying to figure out what I am, aren't you? My mother was human and my father was a troll. Pretty risqué for the times, don't you think? What with the laws prohibiting them from marrying and all—saying it wasn't natural." She smiled and walked toward me. "I can't think of anything more natural than love, can you?"

I shook my head, still trying to wrap my head around the fact that she was part troll.

"Of course, it's a pain filling out the Queen's tax forms each year for my shop. You have to mark what species you belong to and there's still no "other" category." She sighed. "We have a long way to go." She straightened a few bottles on the shelf. "Anyway, what can I do for you, dear? A love spell? A protection potion, perhaps?"

"N-n-no. I don't need to buy anything." The old woman-troll's face fell. "I mean, I will buy something," I added quickly, and watched her face brighten, "but what I really need is information."

"I'll help any way I can. I'm Helga." She grabbed my hand and pumped it up and down.

"I'm Br—I'm Briar." It was as close to a fairytale name as I could conjure in the moment.

She dropped my hand. "No, you're not. I can smell a liar a mile away. What do you want?"

For some reason, I trusted her. Maybe part of it was that she didn't seem at all interested in the gossip taking place outside her shop. Part of it was that I knew what it felt like to be an outsider. I told her my name and prepared to tell her what I did in Liralelle. I didn't need to.

Helga's mouth hung open. She spoke in an excited whisper. "Bree? The one who slays witches?"

I shifted from one foot to the other, suddenly uncomfortable. "Um, yeah, that's me, I guess. Didn't realize the word got around that much."

Helga dropped to her knees. "Thank the stars—you're real! And don't worry none about being found out—most people in these parts buy into whatever the Queen tells 'em. You know, princes are the heroes, princesses need rescued, blah, blah, blah." She tapped her finger to her temple. "Only a few of us like to do the thinking for ourselves rather than leave it to others. Like you." She reached for my hand and kissed it. "You've come to help us."

I tried to extricate my hand from hers. "Well, I've come to try and help. I'm real—it's just that I'm not allowed to be seen in the village for obvious reasons. But honestly, I prefer the forest anyway."

She stood up, animation lighting her face. "Of course, I love the forest myself." She looked around and whispered. "I mark the human box on my tax forms since they pay lower taxes than other species, but I live in the troll village. I've been with my man for years."

It was difficult to imagine Helga living with the trolls. The ones I'd come across were short-tempered, hostile creatures. Helga seemed to read my mind. "They're not as bad as you think—just misunderstood. Imagine if you were considered the ugliest creature alive, and to top it off, you were shorter than everyone else. It's a tough life being a troll."

So maybe the chip on their shoulders was justified, but did they have to be so unlikeable? "I guess," I said. "So, the rumors about discontent—" I gestured toward the huddled masses in the street, "they seem to be true. Why are they upset?"

"Ah, very true," Helga said. "Some of the workers haven't been receiving their pay on time."

I frowned. "That seems more like a problem with the Treasury department, plus, that doesn't seem serious enough to cause this kind of uproar. I mean—"

"Did I say I was finished? Give me a minute, will ya." Helga brushed a gray tendril from her face. "The Queen's servant who carried the payments was ambushed before he reached the workers. But that's not the biggest problem."

I waited for her to continue.

She sighed heavily. "The real problem lies in the girls gone missing."

My blood froze. "I hadn't heard. How many?"

Helga glanced out to the street. "Three so far. All teenage girls. Vanished with not a trace left behind. No one can figure it out."

"And they believe that the witch Muriel is behind it?"

Helga coughed. "So they say. Muriel don't sound much like a proper witch name if you ask me. Anyway, that's all I know." She waved toward the window. "I try to stay out of all that nonsense. Who knows what rubbish they're spewing—I overheard one boy saying he's seen Muriel flying around at night, looking for fresh blood to drink."

I shuddered. I didn't need my nightmares to be any worse than they were. "Well, thanks for your time."

"My pleasure. It's a great honor to meet you." Helga seemed to remember my promise to purchase something and tapped her fingers on the shelf, an expectant look on her face. "With who you're up against, a protection spell might do the trick, hmm?"

Aside from allowing a kind witch to bless my sword when I first became initiated into the Queen's service, I wasn't a big believer in charms and potions. Call me old-fashioned but I'd rather have someone fall in love with me on their own, rather than because they drank a magic liquid. My sword was my protection. I scanned the various items on the shelf, and picked up two stained glass bottles, one blue and one lavender.

I handed them to Helga, who raised an eyebrow when she saw the labels. "These aren't for me. They're for my friends."

Helga chuckled and wrapped my purchases. "Interesting choices. Well, before you leave, check with Mr. Fibbons, the bartender at the inn down the street. He's not the most agreeable sort, but he's sharp as a whip and I imagine he knows more than anyone. After a few drinks, people's tongues get as loose as their purse. If anyone in Liralelle knows anything useful about Muriel, it'd be him."

"Thanks, I'm heading there now." I grasped the brown bag and exited the store.

"Mind yourself," Helga called after me.

I stayed close to the shops, away from the street, but still heard some of the townsfolk muttering to one another. One woman said that she and her children hadn't eaten in days, because she still hadn't received her wages. She'd taken to digging for roots in the forest behind their cottage.

In another group, a woman attempted to console a wailing woman over her missing daughter. "We'll find Evelyn. I promise."

If Muriel was behind the disappearances, I knew the chances of finding Evelyn alive were between slim and none.

I came to *Ye Olde Taverne* and entered. Despite the fact that it was mid-day, the place was dark and dingy thanks to small, dirty windows that hardly let in any light. I pulled the scarf from my head and wound it around my arm. A musty smell hung in the air, and several trolls with large pint glasses hovered around a table in the back. Of course, the trolls would hang out here. I thought of Helga, and chided myself for my thoughts, but sometimes a troll really was a troll.

A large, stocky man with a bushy red beard stood behind the bar.

His eyes drilled into me while he dried a thick glass with a cloth. "What'll it be?"

I approached the bar, somewhat intimidated by his size. "Excuse me, are you Mr. Fibbons? I was told you might have some information about—"

"Maybe you didn't hear me. I said, 'What'll it be?'" He turned away from me to place the glass on a shelf.

Helga hadn't been kidding about his personality. "Oh, I don't drink. I just wanted to talk." Several of the trolls snickered. Helga thought you might—"

The bartender kept his back to me when he spoke. "Helga sent ya? Well, I'm known as Fibb round these parts, and I know a little 'bout a lot of things, but still ... no drink, no talk."

I fingered some of the gold coins I'd brought along in case of an emergency. I held one up in the air, dangling it over the counter. "Maybe this would change your mind," I said loudly.

Fibb whipped around and eyed the coin. Before I could react, he grabbed my hand by the wrist. I gasped. He spoke in a low growl. "Put your gold away, missy. There are folk here who ain't eaten proper in days. They might kill for a bit of coin like this."

I looked over my shoulder, and sure enough, several trolls were pointing and whispering in my direction. The bartender released my hand. "Pint of ale or jigger of whiskey?" he boomed. "It's all I got."

I'd never had either, in this world or the other. When I was eight, Dad had let me have a sip of wine on New Year's Eve. He'd laughed when I spit it right back out again. As I got older and found that nothing excited me the way ballet did, I skipped pretty much every party there was.

I gulped and tried to meet Fibb's eyes. Which drink would make me sound tougher? "Whiskey," I said, and discreetly pushed the coin across to him. He swept it up and tucked it into his shirt.

"Whiskey it is," he said, pouring it into a small dark glass. His eyes sparkled with amusement as he slid the glass across the counter.

I sat and stared at the glass. He crossed his arms across his chest.

"Drink up, little lady. Don't you know bar etiquette—drink first, then talk."

Best to get it all over with at once. I'd once seen someone knock their drink back in one gulp in a movie. How hard could it be? I picked up the glass, a weak smile on my lips. "Cheers," I said.

I tipped the glass into my mouth and swigged the entire contents at once. The liquid burned like fire going down my throat, and I dug my fingernails into the bar stool to keep from gagging. If I asked for a glass of water, I'd probably be laughed right out of the place. After the initial heat, a slow, warming sensation spread through my stomach, which was not entirely unpleasant. I had done it without looking like an idiot. I was so proud of myself that I felt like dancing around the bar, but that would either give me away or make me look like I couldn't handle my liquor.

Fibb leaned across the bar and spoke in a low voice. "Not bad for your first time."

My jaw went slack. "Was it that obvious?"

He shrugged. "To me, but it's my job to know. Just like I bet I know who you are. Prince Edgar was in here drunk and bellyaching a year or so ago 'bout some dark-haired girl who stole his glory. Put it together with some other stories I'd heard about a warrior girl." He eyed me up and down, speaking gruffly. "Don't look like much of a warrior to me, truth be told. So, one drink gets you one question. Choose wisely."

The warmth had already spread from my stomach to my entire body, and I was strangely relaxed. I'd better make it a good question because I wasn't sure I could handle any more of his drinks.

"Okay." I tapped my finger on the bar, trying to think. "What do you know about the witch, Muriel?"

Fibb frowned. "That's a pretty vague question, so I'll respond in kind. I know she's been MIA for years—ever since she killed that little girl's family."

The shock must have registered on my face.

"Well I'll be ..." Fibb ran his hand through his course hair. "Wondered whatever happened to you. Terrible thing to have to go through at such a wee age. I—" He stopped talking and handed a tray of filled pint glasses over to a frail yet hard-looking girl who had appeared at the counter. Heavy black-eyeliner rimmed her eyes and a dark shade of burgundy stained her lips. Her shiny hair was the color of night and looked to be the healthiest thing about her.

He waved her off. "Hurry it up, Snow. You know trolls don't like to wait on their refills."

Snow's eyes met mine and for an instant I saw sadness reflected there, before they hardened again and she smirked at me. She sauntered off with the drinks, her tight clothes barely covering her skin.

My eyes widened. "I can't believe she works here."

Fibb looked offended. "It's better than pimping her on the streets like those perv dwarfs had her doing before. I'll have you know this is a respectable establishment."

"Of course. I just … never mind. What were you saying about Muriel?"

"I told you. I hadn't seen her in a very long time—"

Dread and excitement coursed through me. "Wait. You've seen her?"

He held up the whiskey bottle. "I do believe that's a second question."

This time, the shot went down a little smoother and warmer. A slight fuzziness blurred my thoughts, but I fought for clarity. "You've seen Muriel recently?"

He grinned, displaying a cracked front tooth. "Just yesterday as a matter of fact, but don't none of the townsfolk know about it. It'd get their panties all in a bunch."

A sense of dread shot through me. Was this a set-up? Was he working with her? I reached down to make sure my sword was still at my side. I slid off the stool, steadying myself on the bar. The bartender held up his hands. "Relax. Ain't nothing bad going down in my place. I don't stand for that. You're safe here."

I remained standing. "What did Muriel say?"

"Sshhh," he scolded, putting his finger to his lips. He tipped the bottle toward my glass and refilled it. "That's question number three, right there."

Emboldened by the prior two shots, I let my anger take over. Unfortunately, as my judgment was slightly clouded, it meant that I slammed the third shot and wiped my mouth with the back of my hand. "There, happy—now what did she say to you?" My vision blurred and the room started to spin. I had to get out of here before I fell down. "You know what? Forget it. I'm out of here. I'll find Muriel myself." I staggered toward the door.

"Suit yourself," he said. "But I don't think you'll have to."

"What do you mean?" I asked, turning around too quickly. The room seemed to turn with me and I fought the urge to hold onto the wall.

He definitely looked like he was having a good time with this. "You asked me what she said, right? So, I'm telling you."

I squeezed my eyes shut, but that only made the spinning worse. I opened my eyes again and glared at him. "Then tell me already."

The bartender turned somber. "You won't have to look hard to find Muriel—because she's looking for you. I'm guessing she'll find you first."

I STUMBLED into the main hall after dropping Majestic with Edward in the stables. Rolph grabbed my arm to keep me from falling. Concern blazed on his face. "Sweetie, are you alright?" He put a hand to my forehead to check for fever.

"I'm fine. Just got a little bad news is all," I said, breathing in his face.

He reared his head, making a face. "Good heavens, you're drunk."

I shook my head. "No, not drunk. Had a little whiskey though. I'd be totally fine if things stopped spinning."

Rolph clucked like a mother hen. "How am I supposed to take you to the Queen in this condition?"

His words sobered me up a little, and I pulled away from him. "No, I must see her immediately. I've made my decision."

Rolph announced me in his usual way, but the tension in his voice was evident. With everything going on in Liralelle, I couldn't believe his biggest concern was the state of my sobriety. It turned out not to matter, because the Queen was oblivious. "Bree, so good of you to return so quickly."

"You didn't tell me about the missing girls."

She sighed. "I didn't want to bring it up after what you went through. I wanted to spare you more pain. I assumed that knowing it was Muriel would be enough information." A tear leaked out of her eye. "I wish I had someone else as skilled as you are so I wouldn't have to bring you into this. Does this affect your decision?"

I bowed, eyeing the floor and trying to ignore how inviting it looked and how much I really wanted to curl up and nap. "It does, your Highness."

She eyed me expectantly.

"I wish to return to my world to be with my brother."

The Queen slumped in her chair, appearing crestfallen.

"But I shall return tomorrow, and I will take the job. I will hunt Muriel."

The last thing I saw before she chanted the magic words and pointed her scepter at me, was her tired smile.

6

I barely made it to my locker before first bell and was so tired I couldn't see straight. Rolph had been right about the time differential—mostly. Not much time had passed in my world when Kermit and I reappeared down the street from Ava's house the night before. But it had still been three hours. Three hours from when I should have been home after auditions.

First, I checked my cell, which always died as soon as I reached Liralelle—the "can you hear me now campaign?" would have failed miserably there. My phone had multiple messages from Mom, followed by several from Ava who Mom called when she couldn't reach me. As pissed as Ava had been, her last message said she'd covered for me and said I'd stayed late to study at her place.

My brain was fuzzy from lack of sleep and the whiskey. I tried to recall which book I needed for class. I reached in my backpack and pulled one out, but it fell to the floor. Good thing the auditions were yesterday because I would have been tripping over my feet today. I leaned down for the book but it wasn't there.

"Here you go."

I looked up. Ty Wilder held out my book.

Of course he did. The one day I'd been so tired that I'd gotten up five minutes before I had to leave for school. I hadn't had time for make-up, and "doing my hair" had involved running my fingers through my bangs while driving like a maniac to school.

I took the book and couldn't help but notice that his aftershave smelled really good. "Uh, thanks." I checked the hallway for Catelyn but didn't see her anywhere.

He smiled and those blue eyes pierced mine. "So, I'm not exactly sure what happened at the audition, but Catelyn said she'd earned the day off from school today. I'm sorry if that means things didn't go well for you."

Extreme fatigue dampened my anxiety about being in an actual conversation with Ty. I stared into his baby blues and felt no fear. "A Catelyn-free day would usually make me jump for joy, no offense, but I'm too tired to jump right now."

He grinned at me. "None taken. I know how she can be. Anyway, good luck."

"Thanks, I'm hoping it didn't go as badly as I think." The second bell rang which meant I should be heading toward a class—I just still wasn't sure which class that should be.

"Guess we gotta go," he said and backed up a step. "Hey, you going to Trevor's tonight?"

Oh right, the party Ava begged me to go to. Trevor, who was known more for his sexual conquests than his playing ability, played second-string running back for the football team. He had parties almost every weekend, thanks to his newly divorced mom who spent most of her time in Atlantic City in an attempt to regain her youth. Needless to say, I'd never been to one of his parties and had never had the tiniest desire to attend one—until now.

"Um, I don't know." I walked with Ty down the hall and hoped it would spark a recognition of what class I was supposed to be in. Going to a party would require me to stay awake and I'd promised Her Highness I'd come back tonight. We'd agreed on midnight my time, but if I wasn't at home, the funnel cloud would find me wherever I was. I'm sure a funnel cloud swooping me up from Trevor's living room might cause a little gossip. Plus, I needed some sleep or I'd have no chance against Muriel, assuming I had a chance at all.

Ty nudged my shoulder. "You should come. It'll be fun."

I opened my mouth to ask him if Catelyn would be there, but another voice permeated my mental haze.

"You do realize you're going the wrong way? If you're still going to French Lit, that is." Jay Ashland walked toward me going in the opposite direction I was headed.

I smacked my head with my hand. "French Lit, right! I'll walk with you."

I attempted to smile at Ty, but even smiling required more effort than I could muster. "See ya," I managed.

"Yeah, see you tonight," he said.

I hadn't even said I was going, but he sure seemed confident I'd be there.

Jay raised an eyebrow at me as we walked to class. "I have to hand it the guy. If he can make a girl forget what class she has, then he's got some skills."

"No, that's not why I ... I mean, it's that .... I'm just really tired."

Jay stopped and faced me as we reached the door to class. "Oh wow, yeah, you look like hell."

I glared at him through blood shot eyes. "Thanks, Jay. Just a tip— you'll never make girls forget what class they're in with lines like that."

"Sorry, it's just that I've never seen you this beat. What's going on?" He reached out and tucked a stray piece of uncombed hair behind my ear. I didn't normally like people invading my space but his touch was gentle and his brown eyes looked concerned.

"It's a long story. Basically, I didn't get much, actually any, sleep last night."

The final bell rang and Ms. Rossueau ushered us into class, before Jay could say anything else. I sat close to the back of the room with Jay right behind me. Ms. Rousseau's French accent lulled me into a trance.

Next thing I knew, a hand patted my back and I woke with drool running down the side of my chin.

"Huh?" I blinked and rubbed gunk out of my eye.

The classroom was empty, save for Jay, who stood next to me. I wiped my chin with the sleeve of my shirt, grateful that he was the only one there to witness the drool fest. I reached for my backpack and tried to stand.

Jay grabbed my arm and helped me up. "You slept straight through the bell. I told Ms. Rousseau that you weren't feeling well. It's good you have an A in this class, because she bought it. You sure you shouldn't just go home?"

I slung my backpack over my shoulder. "I'm sure. I'll be fine. Plus, I find out about the auditions after school."

"And you have whatever that thing is with Ty tonight, right?" His deep brown eyes prodded mine.

I crinkled my brow at him. "What? Oh, that's just one of Trevor's parties. I've never been to one so I probably won't go."

Jay walked out into the hall with me. "I've been to a couple, but unless you enjoy loud, drunk people, I wouldn't say you're missing out on much."

I smiled. "When you put it like that, it sounds so tempting."

"See you in Trig," he said and turned down another hall. "And try to stay awake."

FOR THE NEXT TWO CLASSES, I didn't do so great at the staying awake part. In fact, I dozed and napped my way through the entire morning. When the bell for the lunch period rang, my big plan involved catching a nap in my car until Trig class.

Ava intercepted me on my way toward the exit. "Oh my gosh, I've been looking everywhere for you. Are you okay? What happened to you last night?" She thrust her hand on her hip. "I mean, don't get me wrong, I'm still mad at you, but your mom was freaking out with a capital F last night. I covered for you but then wondered if something bad had happened to you and if I should call the police."

"I know." I leaned against a nearby locker. "Look, I'm really, really sorry for bailing so fast last night. I should have been there for you, and I swear I'll make it up to you."

"So, you're not gonna tell me where you were?" Ava's foot tapped against the floor.

I gulped. "I, uh, can't right now."

She frowned at me a second, then looked like a light bulb went off in her head. "I know how you can make it up to me! The party tonight at Trevor's ... don't look at me like that. You owe me, plus I heard Ty's going to be there. Pretty, pretty please." Ava started to get down on her knees in the hall.

"Get up, already," I said and looked around. I didn't want to tell her that Ty already told me he would be there. Even though I was pretty sure he was just being nice, Ava would be devastated if Ty didn't like her back. The fact that I'd crushed on him for years wouldn't matter, because I never said it out loud like she did.

Ava planted her knees on the floor and held her hands up as though in prayer. "Not until you say you'll go to the party with me tonight. Please with a cherry on top."

"Fine, I'll go with you, just get up." I turned just as Jay breezed past us.

He winked at me as he strolled by. "Guess someone's in demand tonight."

Ava eyed me. "What does that mean?"

I shrugged. "Who knows? It's Jay." I tugged on her sleeve to pull her up. "C'mon. Let's grab some lunch."

AVA MET me by Kermit after school. The catnaps during the day had refreshed me enough to be anxious on the way to the studio.

"Don't even worry about it. You so have the lead." Ava chattered the whole way, but I only caught bits and pieces of what she said. My mind raced with mixed up thoughts involving Sam, Her Highness, Muriel, Ava, and Jay.

We pulled into the lot and parked at the far corner by a large tree.

The naked branches swayed as small gusts of cold wind blew through them.

I turned off the car and took a breath. "Ava, before we go in there and find out about the auditions, I wanted you to know that I heard what you said last night. I'm so sorry about your mom and about everything you're going through."

Ava squeezed my hand. "Thanks. I think a party is what we both need right now. You're looking a little ragged yourself. Now let's get in there. If he gave the lead to Catelyn instead of you, I swear I'm up and quitting."

By the time we got inside, girls had already crowded around the sheet posted outside the studio door. Sighs of disappointment and squeals of joy punctuated the otherwise silent room. Catelyn stood off to the side and glared at me.

"No way! That can only mean good news for you," Ava whispered.

Relief swept over me, but I had to see the sheet for myself.

Cary stepped away from the sheet and glanced our way. "Congrats, Bree. You deserve it." She waved me up to see the sheet. The level of her animation told me she was pretty happy with her own results.

Ava took a deep breath and followed. "Yay. I knew you'd get it. Now please let me be a fairy."

Another girl moved over so I could squeeze in. Sure enough, my name was right there at the top of the list:

Princess Aurora—Bree McKenna

A sigh of relief escaped. Until I saw it for myself, I couldn't believe I really had the lead. Right under my name was Catelyn's—she'd gotten the part of Lilac Fairy.

"Oh, schizzlesticks," Ava muttered. She must have seen Catelyn's part too. A second later though, she said, "Whew, at least I'm a fairy."

I scanned down the list and smiled. "Canary Fairy. Congrats!" She might have wanted Lilac, but Canary was the perfect fit for her bubbly personality. Cary had landed the part of Carabosse which explained her excitement level.

Cary even attempted to congratulate Catelyn on her role, but Catelyn responded only with a dramatic eye roll.

"C'mon, Catelyn," another girl said, "Lilac is a great role. We can celebrate at Trevor's tonight."

My stomach dropped. Why would Ty have invited me if she was going to be there? It's not like she would ever allow him to talk to me.

Catelyn scoffed and bit at the edge of her long nail. "I have to babysit my evil little brother tonight."

My heart did a somersault. Catelyn wasn't going tonight. Maybe that's why Ty had asked if I was going. A small voice inside me questioned the integrity of someone looking to play while his girlfriend was away, but that didn't mean I couldn't talk to the guy.

Loud claps echoed in the room. "Are we here to dance or to socialize?" Adrian snapped his fingers and pointed inside the studio. "We have much work to do if you have any hope of putting on a decent performance."

We filed past him into the room. "For those of you who got the parts you wanted, good for you," he said. "And for those who didn't—"

Ava turned and mouthed his favorite words as he said them. "Practice. Do better."

He pressed play and Tchaikovsky filled the room. I couldn't wait until final rehearsals with the actual orchestra. Jay had never seen me dance before. I pondered this thought a second before the music erased everything in my mind except the dance.

"Geez, could he have worked us any harder tonight?" Ava asked as we took off our pointe shoes. "I mean, it was only the first official practice, and now I'm so sweaty I'll have to shower before the party."

The party. As much as I'd love to see Ty outside of school, the two-hour rehearsal had wiped out what little amount of energy I had stored from my naps. Mom would be at work by the time I got home, so the sitter would be there with Cal. I'd have just enough time to put him to bed and catch a few zzzzz's before the midnight tornado came for me. Not to mention I still owed him a game of catch.

"I don't think I can go," I said and yawned for dramatic effect. "I'm so tired, and—"

"Oh, no you don't," Ava interrupted. "Don't think you can get all diva-like just because you're the lead. I told Rae we'd pick her up at nine sharp. You promised."

I pushed open the door and stepped outside. The wind had whipped into a frenzy and dead leaves whizzed past us. One leaf got caught in my hair and I stopped to pull it out. I remembered my mom's saying after another long night shift at the hospital, *'I'll have time enough to sleep when I'm dead.'*

"Maybe if I can catch a nap for an hour, maybe ..."

"You've been napping all day. I don't want to hear it."

Kermit's green glow guided us in the dark. The wind continued to wail and an empty soda can skittered across the parking lot.

Ava pulled her coat tighter around her. It became difficult to walk against the strong winds, and my hair blew straight back from my face.

"Holy cow, I feel like I'm about to blow away," Ava called over the gusting winds. She grabbed onto my arm for support.

"We're almost there," I said, looking again for Kermit. My eyes scanned the darkness but I couldn't see anything for a second. Then I realized why.

A chill passed through me and my heart stopped in my chest. I couldn't see Kermit because between me and my car was a large, shimmering tunnel cloud. The Queen hadn't waited for midnight. I tried to push Ava away from me but the cloud closed in fast. It was too late. It sucked us both in.

7

"What the hell?" Ava looked around. She grabbed my arm even tighter.

One second ago, we'd been in a windy parking lot at night and now we were standing in the sunlit courtyard of a palace. I didn't think it would work to tell her I'd driven her home and she was dreaming.

She faced me, eyes wide, and I worried she might start screaming.

"There you are darling. You won't believe—" Rolph opened the palace door but stopped short at the sight of Ava. He flipped his pink polka-dotted scarf around his neck. "And who do we have here?"

Ava's mouth open and closed like a fish. "What the hell?" she asked again.

Rolph looked back and forth at us.

I was going to be in so much trouble with Her Highness. Bringing an outsider to Liralelle was strictly prohibited. I gulped. "It wasn't my fault. She was holding on to me when I was summoned ... before our scheduled time, I might add."

Rolph's eyes darted around to make sure no one had seen us. He pulled us both inside and quickly locked the door. "This is not good, not good at all. The Queen is going to have a coronary." He put a hand over his own heart. "Unless I have one first."

Ava's face had gone completely white and I hoped she wouldn't faint. I pulled her over to a chair inside the main entrance, sat her down, and pleaded with Rolph. "Maybe the Queen doesn't have to know. No one has seen her. You could keep her here until I'm finished."

Rolph shook his head. "That will never work. If the Queen sends you back, then *she* will be stuck here on her own." He gestured toward Ava.

Ava's eyes looked like they were about to pop out of her skull. Rolph was right. I'd have to tell Her Highness because only she had the power to send someone from one world to another.

Ava stood. "Would somebody please tell me what's going on before I start running?"

Rolph scratched his head. "Maybe the Queen could give her a magic sleep potion before sending her back? She'll think she dreamed this."

"I can hear you. I'm right here." Ava stamped her foot and her voice rose to a squeaky pitch, like she was barely holding on.

"A, I'm so sorry. I don't even know how to explain because it will sound so crazy," I said.

Guards ran out of a door from the chamber down the hall. They raced past us and out the doors, without giving Ava so much as a second glance. One soldier spotted me and called out, "I'd get in there fast if I were you. There's trouble."

Rolph ushered Ava and I toward the Queen's chamber. "No time for explanations now. You'll have to catch your friend up later."

The Queen looked bedraggled, her reddish hair frizzed around her face, like she'd either just woken up or hadn't slept in days. I wasn't sure which since I never knew exactly how much time passed here while I was away.

Her eyes passed over Ava and moved back to me. Whatever it was must be really bad because the fact that Ava didn't belong here didn't seem to register.

"What's going on?" I asked.

Ava gaped at me. "You mean *you* don't even know?"

The Queen's bleary eyes rested on me. "There's been a murder in Liralelle."

There hadn't been a murder here in some time, unless you counted the people I killed, but Her Highness assured me that killing bad people wasn't the same as murder. At least that's what I told myself each time I counted my gold.

The Queen waved her hand. "No one of great importance, but she was one of my subjects and Liralelle is supposed to be a safe place." She stared at me. "I mean, that's why I hired you, Bree."

Did I detect accusation in her voice, like it was my fault someone died because I hadn't killed Muriel fast enough?

"Bree?" Ava whispered in my direction.

"Later," I mumbled through clenched teeth.

Rolph dabbed at his eyes with the end of his scarf. "Poor Helga."

I stiffened. "Helga from the market?"

He nodded. "Ay, the magic shop keeper. Her potions were fabulous."

Though days must have passed in Fairyland, I'd only spoken with Helga hours earlier. She hadn't had contact with Muriel at that point, but the bartender had. Thinking back on my conversation with him, the only thing I learned—aside from the fact that I couldn't hold my whiskey—was that Muriel knew I was in Liralelle. I'd actually liked Helga; she'd made me reconsider my stance on trolls.

The Queen stiffened. "We don't need potions, we need stopping power. I've sent my guards into the market to search high and low for that evil wench." She sank back into her chair. "But as you well know, my guards aren't exactly known for their competence."

If they had been, she wouldn't have needed me in the first place. They suffered from an inverse correlation between the size of their muscles and that of their frontal lobes.

"I need you to find Muriel immediately, before she can do more damage." She waved me off.

I grabbed Ava's arm and turned to leave.

"Wait," the Queen commanded. Her eyes returned to Ava.

Crap.

"Who is this girl?"

I bowed low. "My assistant, your Majesty. I've never faced my family's murderer before. I thought I might need help."

Ava gasped. "Oh my god, your family's been murdered? After the audition? This is so messed up." She started sobbing. "Would somebody please tell me what the holy hell is happening—"

"Shhh." I spun her around and pulled her out of the room, before the Queen could ask anything else. Rolph hurried after us.

I put a finger to Ava's lips. "No, my family in our world isn't dead. My family here is. Give me one sec and I'll try to explain." I whirled around to Rolph. "This murder—are you sure it was Muriel?"

Rolph looked shocked at the question. "Of course, who else would it be?"

Good question. "Okay, I'm taking Ava with me. We'll be back as soon as we can, so I can get her home."

Rolph hugged me. "Be careful, darling. Things are out of control."

He opened the palace door, and I dragged Ava into the courtyard. Several puffy clouds floated across the sky, as two bluebirds danced in the air before landing on a diamond encrusted birdbath decorated with emeralds and rubies. Ava rubbed her eyes. "I seriously think I'm having a breakdown." Tears trickled down her face.

I put my arm around her shoulder and led her to the stable. "You're not. It's okay."

She sniffled but nodded. I helped her mount Majestic and climbed on behind her. She stared down as if she just realized she was on a horse. "Where are we going?"

There was no way to sugar coat it. She'd see for herself soon enough. "Um, the troll village."

Ava gave a laugh that was just shy of hysterical. "Of course."

～

I GAVE her the condensed version as we trotted through the forest, this time veering left toward the troll village. If the guards had gone to the center market, Muriel would have to be dumb as a stone to still be hanging out there. Tree branches swayed along with Majestic's movements, as though granting us passage through them.

Ava turned around to face me several times as I spoke, her mouth gaping in astonishment. She absentmindedly petted Majestic's mane with her hand that wasn't gripping the saddle. When I finished, she blinked slowly. "So, to clarify, you're saying we're in a parallel universe that just happens to be the same Fairytale world we've read about since childhood, except it's really called Liralelle, and oh yeah, nothing is really the same as we were told."

"Pretty much. The PR department thought "Fairyland" sounded prettier than Liralelle. You have to agree with that one, right?" Maybe this wouldn't be so hard on her after all.

Ava's voice rose an octave. "And you, Bree the Earth-sent ballerina, are the one who kills the witches because the princes are really homely cowards."

Uh oh. "Well, that's the gist of it, but I get paid well, and the princesses don't know about me since they're either imprisoned or sheltered. They marry the princes and everyone lives happily ever after. It's a win-win."

"Hold on. I'm still stuck on the part that the woman we're going to find is who murdered your entire 'parallel universe' family. As in, I'm about to get killed, and if I die in this world, I'll probably be gone in my world too, right?" Her speech had reached a shrill pitch.

I slowed Majestic for a minute and put my hand on Ava's shoulder. "Technically, yes, but I'm not going to let that happen."

A sob tore from her throat. "Right, because you're going to plié the witch to death?"

"Ha-ha. No, look." I pulled out my sword from its sheath and waved it in front of her. "I've got other skills in this world."

"Put that thing away." Ava wiped at her eyes. "I still don't understand all this. I mean, how did you end up in our world in the first place?"

"That's a much longer explanation. I—"

"Bree!"

We turned to see Red skipping toward us, her cape flapping behind her.

"Red, what are you doing out here?" I asked. "I told you it was dangerous to be out alone."

She stopped when she reached us and patted Majestic, who snorted in greeting. Red peered up at Ava.

"Hi, I'm Red." Red grinned at me. "Thanks to you, I can run around all I want." She turned to Ava. "Bree gave me the coolest magic potion ever."

I rolled my eyes. "You're welcome, but that's supposed to be for emergencies only."

She reached into her basket and pulled out the blue colored bottle. "But it's so much fun." Red turned to Ava. "Watch this, then tell me if I need to be worried about being in the woods on my own."

Before I could say anything, she'd uncorked the bottle and taken a swig. Her head and body morphed into a ten-foot tall, two-headed snarling monster. Each head contained about one thousand, sharp teeth. The teeth were small but pointed.

Ava jerked back and screamed. Majestic reared up in defense against the monstrosity that had appeared before us. I grabbed onto her reins and tried to calm her.

"Red!" I yelled. "There's only so much in the bottle. Save it for when you really need it!"

A sound like laughter came out of both its mouths, and she waved with a huge, clawed paw, and ran off toward her house, looking like a freakish child-monster.

Ava glanced back at me. "That wasn't, I mean, was that—"

"Little Red Riding Hood?" I finished, nudging a still-fearful Majestic onward. "Yep. Don't worry. That potion I gave her will wear off in an hour, but I wanted her to be able to fend off an attacker, you know?"

We crossed a bridge over a small, but rapidly moving river. I pointed at a small hut in the distance. "That's her house back there."

Ava shook her head and called over her shoulder. "Let me guess.

Over the river and through the woods, so her grandmother's house is back the other way somewhere?"

I frowned. "No, that part never happened. Red's mom was a gypsy who ran away from home as a teenager. Red's never even met her grandma. The Department of Eternal Records thought the grandma-in-peril aspect would gain more sympathy from readers."

"Unbelievable."

"We only have about another half mile before the troll village. That's where Helga, the one who was killed, lived. I want to see if anyone there knows anything."

Another, larger cottage sat nearer to the trail as we rounded a bend in the woods. A white picket fence with peeling paint encircled the yard. Though it looked like it had once been lush and beautiful, the rose bushes had shriveled and the grass had been taken over by weeds. A dwarf sat chain-smoking on the front porch.

"Howdy, pretty ladies" he called out, then bent over and coughed violently.

I waved hesitantly. "That's one of the seven dwarfs," I told Ava.

Her eyes about bugged out of her head. "Which one? Sleepy? Grumpy?"

"I think that one is Doug. They're total jerks, so let's move faster," I whispered to her, and tugged on Majestic's reins.

Ava whispered over her shoulder. "Doug the dwarf? Are you kidding me?"

Doug stood, but barely reached the rail of the the porch. "Ain't you nice gals gonna stop and chat with me?"

"Sorry," I called. "We're really busy today."

He snorted. "Well, if you see Snow, tell her she best be home on time tonight."

I didn't respond as Majestic broke into a faster pace. Before Ava could ask, I leaned up to explain. "She's not called Snow White for her creamy complexion. She's an addict. The dwarfs gave her free 'snow' 'til she was hooked, then they pimped her out to support them. Now she serves drinks at a bar in the village."

Fresh tears welled in Ava's eyes. "I can't believe how different this is from all the fairytales I used to read. This sucks."

"Yeah, I know." The Eternal Records peeps weren't stupid. It's not like parents in my world would have shelled out big bucks for their kids to see a Snow White movie that involved her going down on a dwarf in exchange for drugs. This way, "Fairyland" seemed to be a magical place where bad people were easily defeated. Her Highness got some money out of it too, so she must have had a contact besides me in our world.

The smell of pine hung heavy in the air. When the scent of burning logs mixed with the pine, I knew we'd almost reached the troll village. They were responsible for keeping the fire of Liralelle burning at all times. The job suited them well as they weren't the most social creatures. Thick plumes of smoke drifted skyward, and we got close enough to see the flames licking the air above the giant fire pit. The large gate, fashioned from huge tree trunks, was wide open, though hand-carved *Keep Out* signs lined the entrance.

"Are you sure we should be here?" Ava asked. "I mean, aren't the trolls dangerous?"

I looked up at the gate I'd only entered a handful of times. "Not so much dangerous as perpetually cranky."

I guided Majestic to the hitching post by the gate, and eased Ava down. There was an empty bucket and water pump, so I pumped some water for the horse and patted her. "We'll be right back." I pulled Ava through the gate. "Come on."

Several trolls lumbered toward the fire pit carrying a large log on their shoulders. One glanced at us and muttered something under his breath before moving on. The rest were either very focused on the logs or very focused on ignoring us. This was not going to be fun.

The perimeter of the area contained small wooden dwellings. Female trolls batted rugs over the clotheslines, while even smaller troll children chased each other with wooden clubs. Maybe a female would be more helpful. We skirted the fire pit and approached a dwelling where a woman brushed pine needles out the front door of her house with a stiff broom.

Though she had to see me coming, she didn't acknowledge me until I stepped onto her porch. "What'cha want?"

I'd killed too many evil villains to count, yet these trolls managed to intimidate me every time. "I'm Bree, and this is Ava—"

"Don't care what'cha call yourselves. What'cha want?" She scowled at us, holding the broom upright now, other hand on her hip.

Ava took a step back until she was behind me. A boy troll ran by and clubbed another boy on the head. The boy fell down, holding his head in his hand. Ava moved toward the injured boy. "Are you okay?"

The woman swatted at Ava with the broom. "Leave him alone, will ya. 'Course he's okay. They're just playin' around ... their heads won't toughen up on their own, you know."

Ava jumped back from the troll's broom. The boy troll jumped up from the ground, shook his head back and forth, and started swinging his own club at the boy who had hit him. "You're dead," he yelled.

The smaller one laughed and ran off into the woods. "You have to catch me first."

I swallowed and looked back at the woman. "I'm looking for Helga's, ah, husband."

Her black, beady eyes narrowed. "He ain't no husband of hers. Gotta be the same species for a marriage to be legal in these parts. She didn't never belong here. She's dead, you know? Had it coming, you ask me."

This was not going smoothly. "I know she's dead—that's why I'm here." Being nice wasn't getting me anywhere. I stood up straighter, fingering my sword. "Do you know her man or not?"

The woman scowled but pointed a knotty finger toward the far side of the fire pit. "He's over yonder. Do me a favor, will ya?" She stepped back into her house. "Don't tell him it was me that sent ya." She slammed the door in my face.

I swiveled to face Ava. "That went well."

"Oh my gosh, I can't even believe how mean she was to us ... no manners whatsoever. And those boys are total barbarians. This place is crazy on a stick."

I laughed. "I don't even know what that means, but I'm glad you're talking again. Come on, let's get this over with."

We crossed the clearing surrounding the fire pit, where several muscular trolls took turns tossing logs onto the fire. Ava leaned over. "I would totally die of boredom if that was my job. Though my arms would get really buff."

A troll stopped and stroked his long, red beard while looking Ava up and down. "Don't see many that look like you 'round these parts." He reached a hand toward Ava's curls.

"Don't even think about it, buddy." She jerked her head away from his hand.

He held up both hands. "I meant no harm, miss. Your hair is real purty is all."

Ava blushed. "Thank you, but where I come from, people don't touch other people without their permission."

The troll nodded. "Oh." He reached his hand out again. "Might I have permission to touch your hair?" His fingers wrapped around a lock before she could respond. "Wow, it's so soft."

Ava's blush deepened. "Thank you. Okay, then. Well, we gotta get going." She took a step backward, and as her hair pulled from his grasp, she tripped over a tree root.

He reached an arm around her waist and caught her before she hit the ground. "Careful there, miss."

Ava tucked her hair behind her ear and extracted herself from the troll's grip. "Thanks again." She tugged on my sleeve. "Let's go find that troll."

I tried not to giggle as we headed toward the hut on the far side of the pit.

The troll called after us. "Name's Travis, should you need it, miss."

Ava waved her hand in the air but didn't respond. "Don't say anything," she said sideways through her mouth. "I mean it."

I mock-zipped my lips but couldn't stop chuckling. The hut was less than twenty feet away, and it already seemed different than the others. More cheerful. The area around the hut appeared neat and tidy, with flower baskets hung underneath the windows. A male troll stood next to the house, as he watered roses that climbed a white trellis up the side of the hut. He looked over.

I nodded at the huge pink blooms. "Your roses are gorgeous."

He smiled, but it didn't reach his eyes. The small watering can seemed heavy in his hand. "Thank you. These were my wife's pride and joy."

"Helga was your wife then?"

His face grew harder. "Yes, she was. Helga von Herbert. I'm Horace Herbert. Don't care 'bout what others think marriage is. I loved her more than I loved life itself. If that isn't real marriage, then I don't know what is." A tear rolled down his cheek.

Ava nudged me to say something, but I wasn't sure what to say. Consoling people was much harder than killing them.

She sighed in exasperation and moved to pat his back. "I'm so sorry, Horace," Ava said. "I can't imagine how horrible it must be to lose someone you love."

I was an expert in the subject but couldn't seem to convey any helpful sentiments.

Horace studied me and the sword at my side, and his eyes narrowed. "What do you want anyway?"

Ava smiled at Horace. "Oh, she just spoke to Helga not long ago. Right?"

Horace reached quickly toward a bush and pulled out a large club. Ava cringed and froze like a frightened deer.

I put my hands up in the air. "No, not recently, I don't know how long ago I spoke to her. I'm from, uh, somewhere else."

Why the hell was I still keeping my identity a secret? After I found Muriel, I'd avenge my family and get all the money I'd need for Juilliard. I'd be done with this place.

He didn't put the club down. "That don't make sense to me. What do you mean somewhere else?"

I ran a hand through my dark hair. "It's complicated."

His grip tightened on the weapon and he raised it an inch. "You've got about a minute to simplify it for me."

I backed away a step to show I wasn't a threat. "I'm Bree. I'm from a different place—a parallel universe basically. The Queen hires me to take out undesirables. But time runs differently in my world so I don't know how long ago I spoke with Helga. It was at her shop in the village."

Horace relaxed his grip on the club. "Bree." He nodded. "Helga told me about you coming in her shop. It was three nights ago." His eyes moved side to side. "We shouldn't talk out here. Please come in and take tea with me."

Ava shot me a questioning look with her eyes, and I shrugged and followed Horace into the hut. Ava followed. A circular, braided rug lay in the center of the small main room. A kettle hung over the hearth where wood burned in the fireplace. The heat permeated the room, making the atmosphere cozy and warm. Horace gestured for us to sit at a square wooden table set with four chairs. Several photographs hung on the walls. One portrayed Helga laughing at something beyond the frame of the picture. The laugh lit her up, making her face appear years younger, her white hair the only telltale sign of advanced age. Horace followed my eyes to the wall.

"She looks happy," I said.

He smiled, a real smile this time. "She was happy. A breath of fresh air in a village filled with grumpy old trolls like us. Sure, a few of the gals here thought she didn't belong—that she had no right taking away a perfectly eligible troll from them."

Ava rolled her eyes. "Yeah, I think we met one of those across the way." She jerked her thumb toward the window facing the troll we'd spoken with earlier.

He chuckled. "Yes, that old bird, Hildegard. She couldn't catch herself a male troll with a steel trap and chains. Most here aren't as bad as that. Helga had a lot of friends here ... she had a way of making you smile." The scent of lilac and vanilla filled the room—it was the most intoxicating tea I'd ever smelled.

Horace poured tea into the cups and water splashed over the sides. "Sorry, Helga usually did this part. I'm a little clumsy."

Ava dried the table with a cloth napkin. "No worries. It's fine, thank you, Horace."

I raised an eyebrow at her. "You've adjusted quickly. You'd think you went to parallel universes every day after school."

Ava lifted the teacup to her lip and blew on it. "Just going with the flow. Anyway, I'm still not convinced I'm not hallucinating and experiencing a total breakdown. I'm just going to enjoy this tea for now, thank you."

Horace's eyebrows knitted together in apparent confusion.

"She's here by accident," I explained, but the look on his face told me I hadn't explained anything. "Anyway, about Helga. We didn't talk long, but I asked her about Muriel. She hadn't seen her but had heard rumors."

Horace's face darkened and he pounded the table, causing tea to spill everywhere. "Helga saw that witch woman sure enough, it was the night after you'd visited. Helga came home talkin' a blue streak 'bout how you were going to save us, talkin' about them missing children. I told her she might do best takin' a few days off work—keep her away from the chaos 'til things settled down a bit." He pulled at his dark beard. "She never made it back to work. Muriel came that night."

I closed my eyes, trying to keep the flashbacks away, trying not to think of the brother I'd lost. "Did she ..." I forced the words out, "kill Helga here?"

Horace punched a fist into his other hand. "No. No one could do that to my Helga with me there. The old woman knocked on the door late that night. I didn't know who she was until later. I was back in the bedroom and when I came out, she was whispering in Helga's ear. I didn't like the looks of her and asked who she was." Horace swallowed and his jaw clenched. "I'll never forget when she looked directly at me ... those eyes. Pale and watery, they were."

The image of Muriel's eyes came back clear as day, eyes that bored into me as she stood over my little brother's body. My voice came out barely above a whisper. "And?"

"She just turned and disappeared back into the night. Helga looked shaken to the core. I asked her who that woman was, and she told me it was Muriel." He shook his head. "Imagine. We'd all heard about the atrocities committed by her, and I find out that the most evil witch in Liralelle had just been on our doorstep. I ran outside, but she was nowhere to be found. It was like she turned into the dark itself."

Ava put her tea down, eyes darting around the room, as though worried Muriel might pop out at any moment. She took another large slurp of tea and slumped back in her seat. "This is the best tea ever."

Horace scratched his head. "I locked the door and told Helga to get me if anyone knocked on the door again. She told me she didn't know what Muriel wanted. I woke up the next morning and Helga was gone. There was a note on this here table." He pointed to the specific spot on the table where the note must have been. "She wrote that she knew I wouldn't have given permission, but that when Muriel had come to the house, she'd asked Helga to meet her in the woods. Helga must have snuck out to meet her."

He looked out the window toward the denser part of the forest beyond the fire pit. "A few trolls found her body early in the morning while gathering logs for the fire." Horace's gaze turned back to me. "I still don't understand. Why would Helga have gone with her? She was smarter than that. She hadn't even taken any of her protection spells with her."

"I'm sorry," I said. What else could I say? Truth be told, she should have been smarter than that. I'd only been a child at the time, but I knew enough to run screaming from Muriel when she'd beckoned me with her bony finger. I finally took a small sip of the tea, and the vanilla warmth slid down my throat, erasing my fear. I stared down at the cup and then at Ava's super relaxed demeanor. "Is this tea charmed?"

Horace looked puzzled, then laughed. "Must be. Helga told me I was too much of a worrier. She was always putting spells on things to get me to relax. Sorry 'bout that."

Ava drained the last of her cup. "You could make so much money off this stuff in our world. It's like liquid Xanax." She sat up straighter. "I mean, not that I'd know."

I frowned and pushed my chair back. Once things were back to normal, Ava and I were going to have a serious chat.

"Thanks for talking to us, Horace." I stood and looked out toward the woods where Helga's body had been found. "I don't suppose anyone heard anything that night?"

Horace slowly shook his head. "Nothing. And I've asked everyone. You'll find Muriel, won't you? You'll kill her so she can't hurt someone else the way she hurt my Helga?"

The witch had caused more pain to me and others than anyone I'd known. "Yes, I'll find her, Horace."

I reached out to pat his arm, but Ava embraced him in a huge hug. "You poor, poor man. Don't you worry, Bree will kill that witch. I'm her helper, you know. Like a sidekick."

We walked toward the woods behind the fire pit, ignoring the stares of various trolls. "My sidekick? Are you kidding?"

"I'm here, aren't I? I can't just sit and twiddle my thumbs while you're off fighting evil. Besides, this is so much more exciting than school, you know?"

I stared at her. "No more tea for you. Seriously, I'm worried about you."

Ava laughed. "Don't be. If I'm not having a breakdown, this is the creepiest, coolest thing I've been part of. Let me guess. We're going to look for clues in the woods, right?"

"Right." I sighed. "But then we have to get back to Majestic and the palace. We need to figure out a way to get home. We've been gone longer than usual. I'm usually in-and-out, so to speak, so we'll have to finish up later."

THE WOODS WERE QUIET, not even a slight breeze rustling the trees. The workers at the fire pit couldn't be heard from deep in the forest. The further we traveled inward, the greater the silence. Even the birds ceased chattering after awhile.

"What exactly are we looking for?" Ava whispered.

"Anything unusual. Anything out of place." A knotted pine, taller than all the others, caught my eye. It towered over the forest, almost like a beacon. A tangled knot of roots poked through the ground around it and I stepped carefully over them. A slim ray of sunlight penetrated the foliage near the base of the tree. Something small sparkled. Ava inspected some nearby rocks, like she was part of a crime detective show. I crept over to the sparkling object and leaned over for a better look. It glittered like a miniature sun. I reached down and scooped it up. It was the most beautiful thing I'd seen.

It was also familiar. I slid it into my pocket.

"All I'm finding is dirt and more dirt," Ava whined across the space. "Did you find anything?"

I didn't want to speak yet, because I wanted to be sure. "Maybe, but we should get back."

She kicked the smallest rock under her. "Some helper I'm turning out to be. I can come back with you, right?"

No, the hell you can't. "We'll see."

WE HURRIED BACK TO MAJESTIC, steering clear of Hildegard's boys who continued to beat each other over the head with clubs. As soon as we crossed the bridge by Red's house, we heard singing. A sweet, crystal clear voice cut through the silence. A girl with long, flowing hair swirled in circles with outstretched arms.

"Holy amaze balls," said Ava. "That's Sleeping Beauty, Princess Aurora, isn't it? She's the part you have in the recital."

"Yep."

"She's singing just the way she does in the story. Her voice is amazing." A bird zoomed by us, heading away from the princess toward the woods. "Let me guess, that's not the whole story either."

I shook my head. "But really, who wouldn't go a little soft in the head after being isolated in the woods for sixteen years? She thinks the birds sing back to her, but all the animals run in the opposite direction when they hear her. They just want some peace and quiet, and she won't leave them alone."

Ava went quiet, seemingly lost in thought for the next half mile.

Then she blurted out what had apparently been bothering her. "They're really not cute at all? The princes, I mean?"

"Nope. Nothing like the pictures in the books."

Ava groaned. "That's so sad. At least when I thought fairytales weren't real, I could daydream about handsome princes riding on white stallions." She pointed an accusatory finger at me. "You've killed that dream for me, forever."

As though on cue, the thunder of horse hooves beat toward us, and a large black stallion reared when it saw us. It wore a saddle but no rider. Majestic whinnied and started to buck.

A boy burst through the trees. "Archibald! Halt!"

The horse settled back onto four legs again, barely a foot away from us, as it snorted with nostrils flared. Ava trembled as Majestic appeared to be on the verge of a panic attack.

"There, there, it's okay girl." I patted Majestic's side. The boy, dressed in fine clothes, took his horse by the reins with confidence and I couldn't help but notice his muscular build. He looked more man than boy upon closer inspection, probably about our age. His sandy blond hair complimented the blue of his eyes. Overall, he looked like a hotter, stronger version of Ty Wilder. I'd never seen anyone who looked like this in all of Liralelle.

"Sorry about that." He stroked his horse to continue calming it. "I'd just led her to the stream for some water, when Beauty started singing. Archibald can't stand it, and took off. I'm really sorry." He shook his head. "Seems my horse has more sense than my parents—they're still pushing me to marry Beauty. As if getting married could make her sane again."

Ava scoffed. "Marriage is the last thing that would make someone sane."

I glanced at her. Maybe she needed therapy when we got back. Maybe Rae's mom could help her out.

Ava crossed her arms. "Wait, Aurora's a princess. I thought only princes could marry princesses."

He grinned at Ava, revealing perfectly straight, white teeth. What was it with me and teeth? "Guess I'm not like most of the others around here, but I am, in fact, a prince. Prince Evan to be exact." He bowed low with a sweeping gesture. "At your service."

Ava giggled in front of me. She had to be blushing. "I'm Ava."

He sauntered up to Majestic and rubbed her mane, his hand close to where Ava's leg hung from the saddle. "Hi, beautiful girl." Majestic nuzzled his hand as though she'd forgiven the fact that his horse had just charged her. Prince Evan then lifted Ava's hand and pressed it to his mouth. "Pleased to meet you, Ava."

Then he reached behind her and grasped my hand, gazing deep into my eyes. His mouth twitched. "And you, my lady?"

"Bree," I managed.

His eyebrows lifted in surprise. "Ah yes, the warrior." Good thing I'd decided to come clean, because my identity didn't seem so secret these days. News traveled fast, whether good or bad. His eyes traveled down to my sword, then came back up slowly until he met my eyes again. "I've never seen a warrior look like you."

Heat burned my cheeks, but I wouldn't let him fluster me. "And I've never seen a prince look like you."

"Touché." He smiled again, then looked closer. "You look familiar. Have I met you before?"

"Definitely not, Prince Evan," I said. "And why is that, being that I know who most of the princes are around these parts?"

"Just Evan will do." He glanced around. "I keep mainly to the woods. You could say I've been in hiding, but I've also been training. I'm going to find Muriel."

My defenses flew up. Did he think he could just take over my territory? Hot or not, I wasn't about to let a boy take over from here. This job was personal to me. "No, *I'm* going to find Muriel." I flung my hair over my shoulder. "In fact, I've been hired to find her."

Evan looked puzzled. "You're being paid to find Muriel? That's weird." He stood straighter. "Well, I'm not doing it for money. I'm doing it because the witch has it coming to her." He hopped up onto Archibald in one fluid movement and grabbed the reins in both hands. "I guess we'll have to see who finds her first. Good hunting."

With that, he snapped the reins, and Archibald thundered off, leaving nothing but a cloud of dust swirling around us.

I shook my head in disgust. "Unbelievable."

Ava stared after him. "He was pretty unbelievable, wasn't he?" She pivoted around to glare at me. "And you're an unbelievable liar. What, did you want to keep him all for yourself? Not that I'd blame you. I wouldn't share that either."

I sighed and signaled for Majestic to continue toward the castle. "No, I swear I've never seen him before in my life. I didn't even know he existed."

"Sure, and I'm a princess." Ava twirled her hair. "I'd be his princess anyway, that's for sure."

I wound my finger into her curls. "I'm sure he'd love your soft hair as much as Travis."

"Stop it," she said, before giggling again. "I got hit on by a troll—who would have thunk?"

～

ROLPH JUMPED up and down when he saw us, clapping his hands together. He ran down the front steps of the castle entrance. "You're safe! You've been gone so long, I thought something dreadful had happened. Are you okay? The Queen had to be medicated, she was so upset. She's laying down in her chambers, but I'll go get her."

I held up my hand. "No, don't." I pulled him behind a large rose-bush in the courtyard, making sure no guards could see us. Ava ducked behind some lilacs.

I grasped Rolph's hand in mine and spoke in a low voice. "Look, Ava and I need to get home. I know the Queen won't allow us to leave until we find Muriel, so I'm hoping you can help us get home without her knowing."

Rolph's eyes widened. "But we'd need her crown and scepter. No one touches those but her." He wrung his hands. "She'd know I helped you and would have my head."

"No, I've thought it out. She'd never know we were gone. You'd send us home but tell her you hadn't heard anything from us, and then tonight, you'd bring us back again."

Rolph gasped. "I'd have to steal her crown *twice*? Holy hobbits, that's crazy!"

Ava startled at the outburst and held a finger to her lips.

"Shhhhh!" I covered his mouth with my hand. "You can do it, Rolph. I wouldn't ask you if it wasn't super important."

A guard walked through the courtyard in front of the castle. He glanced around before he continued his rounds around the perimeter of the stone walls.

"Now!" I motioned to Ava and pulled on Rolph's arm. We ran toward the castle entrance and made it in the door without anyone noticing.

"Great. We're inside," said Rolph, bent over and breathing hard. "Now what?"

"Didn't you say the Queen was medicated, as in deeply asleep?" I asked.

Rolph groaned. "Did I say that?"

Ava nodded. "Yep, I heard you."

"Then this would be a great time for some crown and scepter borrowing," I said.

Rolph sighed. "Okay, I'll do it." He shook a finger at me. "But only this one time ... well, two times. Can you at least tell me why?"

I debated telling him the whole truth but settled for half. "I'm worried about my brother. I've never been gone this long and I can't concentrate on finding Muriel until I know he's okay."

Rolph grumbled something under his breath but told us to wait in the small sitting room to the left of the entrance. "And don't let anyone see you or this plan is nixed." He left to retrieve the items from the Queen's chamber.

We crept into the cozy but luxurious room and sank onto plush velvet chairs.

Ava smiled. "This has been the craziest day of my life. I just know I'm going to wake up and find out it was all a dream, like Dorothy in Oz."

"I hope you do think it's all a dream. Then I won't feel so badly about bringing you into this."

Rolph returned a few minutes later, breathing hard. He held the crown and scepter away from his body, like he would burst into flames if they got too close. "I can't believe I'm doing this. I'm going to be in so much trouble."

"Just help us already before you hyperventilate." I strained to get a better look at the objects in his hand. "Come closer, Rolph."

Ava sat up straighter in her chair. "What do I do? Just sit here?"

Fear contorted Rolph's face. "Like I've ever done this before. I mean ... I've seen her Majesty do it, but I'm not sure I know exactly what to do."

I waved Ava over to my chair. "I think we have to be touching, A, because that's how you ended up here in the first place." Ava perched on the arm of my chair and linked her arm through mine.

Rolph was only a step away. I fingered the cold stone in my pocket and studied the crown. I've stared at the intricate pattern of stones on the Queen's crown many times while she was bringing me up to speed on my latest job. The stone in my pocket was citrine, a sparkling yellow crystal. This one's cut and high brilliance was exactly like the ones I'd seen before on her crown. I was almost positive that the stone in my pocket was one of two citrines that flanked the huge flawless diamond in the center of her crown. It would mean Her Highness had been in the woods the night Helga was killed. But no, the Queen's jewels were intact, which meant I had squat.

The scepter was within my grasp, but unlike the large stones of the crown, its surface was covered with what looked like thousands of tiny jewels.

Rolph held the crown backwards in his hand, still keeping it as far as possible from him. He pointed the scepter at us and repeated what he'd heard the Queen say numerous times in the past. "Return to your world far from here, but hold your love for Liralelle near."

Nothing happened.

I blinked. "I think you have to wear the crown for it to work, Rolph."

He muttered again, but finally turned the crown and placed it on his head. I sucked in my breath. It didn't make sense. The crown's citrine wasn't missing. Even if Her Highness had lost a stone in the woods, she couldn't have had it replaced so quickly. It's not like perfectly cut citrines grew on trees, even in Liralelle.

Before I had time to ponder it further, Rolph repeated his words. I exhaled in relief at the same time Ava yelped at the sight of the huge black tornado in front of us.

8

The funnel deposited us a few feet away from Kermit in the now empty ballet studio parking lot. The wind had died down to a mere whisper. I tried to think of how I could make Ava think this had all been a trippy dream. Maybe I could tell her that someone put psychedelics in our water bottles.

I fumbled for the keys in my bag and opened the driver side door. "Well, here we are. Hop in."

Ava stared at me as walked around the car and waited for me to unlock her door. She waited until I started the car and pulled out her cell phone to check for reception. "Whoa, it's almost nine. I told Rae we'd pick her up for the party. I can't believe we've only been gone several hours ... it seemed like we were there forever."

I swallowed hard. This wouldn't work, but I had to try. "We were where forever? Look, I don't feel in the mood for a party, so how about I just drop you off and—"

"No!" Ava put up her hand to stop me. "Don't even try it. That was the freakiest thing that's ever happened to me. You can't take it away from me, or make me think it didn't happen, so don't even try. I need this right now." Her lower lip trembled.

I sighed. "Fine, okay, I get it ... sort of. But you can't tell anyone about this, okay? Not even Rae."

Ava pretended to lock her lips with a key. "I won't. But I want to go back with you next time."

I shook my head and turned up the heat in the car. "No way. It's too dangerous and I can't risk you getting hurt. Besides, you'd have to be touching me when the funnel came back, and being glued to my side constantly would be hard to explain, don' cha think?"

Ava crossed her arms over her chest. "Not for best friends, it wouldn't. Plus, it's my condition for staying silent." She stared straight ahead. "As far as getting hurt, I might not be a sword ninja like you, but I take kick-boxing classes at the rec center. I'm sure I could take down a troll if I wanted."

The thought of Ava dropping a troll made me laugh. "Stop it, I shouldn't be encouraging this."

Ava tugged on my arm. "Hey, turn up there for Rae's house."

I raised an eyebrow. "You don't seriously think we're going to a party right now, do you? My mom would ... oh crap, my mom is going to kill me."

I fished for my phone and called her at work. She didn't answer but I knew she was already on the floor at the hospital. I left a message saying I had celebrated with Ava after finding out the audition results, which was why I didn't get home earlier. Then I called the sitter and told her I'd be home in about an hour. She said Cal had gone to bed fine but complained I hadn't been there to kiss him goodnight. Pangs of guilt stabbed at me, but I'd be home when he woke up in the morning.

Ava pulled on the wheel to make it turn right onto Rae's street. I pulled into her driveway and Ava texted her to meet us outside.

"Listen," I said, "We'll take Rae to the party but she'll have to find her own way home. I need some sleep."

The door to Rae's house opened. She flounced out in a gauzy floor length peasant skirt paired with a tank top adorned by a clunky necklace. Somehow, she managed to look effortless and fashionable at the same time. It wasn't fair. Her mom waved to us from the doorway.

"Must be nice to have a mother who cares when you're leaving the house," Ava muttered.

Rae hopped into the back seat. "Evening, ladies. Ready for some fun?"

"Bree's not feeling the fun tonight, right B?" Ava turned to me. "So, I think we might just drop you off."

"What? No way!" Rae pushed between the two front seats, and nudged Ava. "You realize Ty's going to be there? You can't expect a guy like that to be on his own for long." She turned in my direction. "What gives?"

I shrugged. "Tired, I guess. Sorry to be lame, but I'd just fall asleep." I reached the end of her street. "Also, I have no idea where I'm going. Can someone help me out here?"

Ava whipped the phone from her lap. "I'll GPS it. No worries." I wondered if she was trying to prove that she'd be a useful sidekick but then realized that she'd always been helpful like that. If someone had to follow me to Liralelle, I'm glad it was her.

Rae shook her head and sank back into the back seat. "I can't believe you guys are serious. Just stay a few minutes, and then we'll leave. Besides, I brought refreshments." She pulled out a small silver flask that must have been tucked in the waistband of her skirt. "I know you girls don't drink but you're missing out." She tipped it into her mouth and took a long sip. The smell from the flask brought back flashbacks of my whiskey shots, and I knew I wasn't missing out on anything. I tried not to gag.

Ava grabbed the flask from her. "Think I will have some. Maybe I need to be more adventurous." Ava took a long sip, coughed, and handed it back to Rae. "Don't think your mother would approve of this, huh?"

Rae sat up and broke into her mother's professional tone. "Teens who use marijuana are five times more likely to have sex than those who don't." She relaxed her posture and raised the flask. "So, no MJ. I'm drinking instead."

Ava and I needed to have another talk. Between what was going on at home and Liralelle, she was worrying me. I followed Ava's directions to Trevor's house, and hoped we could just drop off Rae without having to talk to anyone. I didn't need the rearview mirror to know that I must look like hell. Ava took several more long pulls from Rae's flask which made me glad we weren't staying at the party. Since she didn't usually drink, I wondered how well she could keep secrets if she got plastered.

We pulled onto Trevor's street and a throng of people gathered in front of his house.

Ava tapped on the window. "Holy hobbits, that's a lot of people."

Rae laughed and spit out the whiskey in her mouth. "Holy hobbits? Is that your new curse word? Oh, I've got a good one. Galloping Gollum!"

Ava clasped her hand over her mouth, like she wanted to take back what she said. Yeah, it was really good we weren't staying.

Rae continued to giggle and spew out Tolkien-inspired swear words. I navigated the car through a group of people and pulled over to the side of the road a little too eagerly. The tire groaned against the curb.

"Freakin' Frodo," Rae exclaimed while bracing herself against the door. Ava erupted into laughter and ignored my death stare.

"Everything okay here, ladies?"

I rolled my window down and stared up into familiar eyes. "Yeah, just a slight parking miscalculation."

"Ty!" Ava squealed beside me. "You're here."

The liquor had evidently brought out her astute observational side.

Ava reached up and tilted the flask out the window. "Here, Ty. Want some?" She shook the flask a minute. "Oh wait, never mind, it's gone."

He smiled and raised an eyebrow at me. "Um, there's more to drink inside if you all want some."

My stomach did a flip-flop at that smile. "Thanks, but, we're just um ..."

Ava bolted out of her door. "We'd love something to drink. I'm parched. Are you parched, Rae?"

"Definitely parched," Rae agreed and stumbled out of the car. They linked arms with Ty on either side.

"Ava, we really need to go," I said.

She wouldn't meet my eyes. "Just one drink. Then we'll go. Promise."

There was no way I could leave her here. She was so tipsy already —there was no way I could trust her to keep quiet. Plus, I couldn't leave my friends drunk at a party without a safe way home.

Rae and Ava laughed and pulled Ty along with them toward Trevor's house. This was not going to be fun. I followed them up the steps and into the house.

The music inside sounded like a combination of rap and rock. It couldn't be any further from my beloved classical music if it tried. I wanted to go home. The three of them beelined to the kitchen, and I felt like a puppy following its inebriated master.

Ty pulled two bottles of beer from an ice chest, popped the tops off with a bottle opener and handed them to Rae and Ava.

"So fancy," Ava giggled.

"Yeah," added Rae. "No plastic cups for this crowd."

Ty looked over the top of Ava's head at me. "Want anything, Bree?"

Yes, you, with a bow on top. "No, thanks. Maybe water."

He rummaged through the cupboard to find a glass. I held up a finger and mouthed "one drink" to Ava. She just smiled. She and Rae raised their bottles in a toast toward me, then clinked them together and drank. At least we'd be leaving sooner rather than later if she drank quickly.

Ty pushed the cup under the fridge dispenser. He handed the cup to me. "Fresh water for the prima ballerina."

I blushed.

"Come on, guys, let's mingle." Rae appeared at my side, flanked by Ava. "You too, Ty. You need to show us around...we've never been to Trevor's before."

They herded him out toward the back porch where people hung out in groups. The smell of pot hung heavy in the air.

"My mother would so not approve of this," Rae said. She and Ava dissolved into laughter again and wondered into the yard.

Ty looked confused, but I shook my head. "It's better if you don't ask."

He stepped back and leaned against the wall of the house. "Congrats on being Princess Aurora. That's awesome."

"Thanks." I moved a smidge closer to him. Surely, it wouldn't hurt anyone if I talked to him. That wasn't breaking any code of friendship. I looked over at Ava who was deep in conversation with a girl from homeroom. "Is Catelyn upset about it?"

I wanted to smack myself. He was finally somewhere without Catelyn Grey, and here I go, reminding him about his girlfriend.

"She's okay." He looked at me with a glint in his eye.

I laughed. "No, she's not. She's mad as hell, isn't she?"

"Maybe a little." He smiled again and my stomach fluttered.

"Hey, B, we'll be right back. I need, um, something." Ava called over to me. "Come on, Rae."

"Just a sec." Rae ran over and shoved her empty flask into the front pocket of my cargo pants. "Hold this for me, please. It keeps slipping in my waistband and I don't want to lose it. It's real silver. Thanks." Without waiting for a response, she disappeared into the house with Ava. Great. They had to be getting more drinks.

Ty grinned at me. "They're hilarious."

"They're something, all right." I was totally going to kill them when we got in the car.

"Ty-man, get your ass over here. We need you on the team."

Trevor stood on the grass with some other guys playing lawn darts. Probably not the best game to play under dim lights while drinking, but who was I to judge.

Ty waved at his friend. "In a minute. Start without me."

Trevor looked from me to Ty. "Right. Got it."

I shuffled my feet and tried to think of something non-dorky to say.

Ty spoke first. "Look, I know we haven't talked a lot before, but I wanted you to know that I think you're pretty cool. I wondered if—"

"Ava likes you," I blurted.

Having a crush on him seemed innocent before—like lusting after a celebrity who didn't know you existed anyway. The possibility that he was one sentence away from asking me out made my heart soar and my stomach sink at the same time.

Stealing him away from Catelyn would be one thing, but I couldn't hurt Ava. No guy was worth that—not even Ty Wilder.

He stepped closer to me and leaned in so his forehead was almost touching mine. He brushed my arm with his finger. "That's nice, but what if I like you?"

"Wanna tell me what's going on here?"

Crap. Ava had reappeared with her brand new drink. Rae stepped out the door behind her, a beer in each hand, and did a double take. I took a step away from Ty like that could negate the fact we'd been an inch apart a second earlier.

"N-n-nothing, he was just telling me something."

Ava thrust her hand on her hip, or attempted to, but missed her hip due to her drunken state. "Yeah, so I heard. He told you that he liked you." Her voice grew louder. "Some friend you are."

Rae put her hand on Ava's arm, but Ava shook her off. Tears filled her eyes. "Just when I thought my life couldn't get any crappier—I should have expected this."

Please don't let her say anything about Liralelle. "It's not what it looks like, Ava."

"Stop, just stop. I'm not stupid, you know." She whirled on Ty. "And as for you, I don't like you anymore. I think you're a ... you're a..."

Don't say it.

"You're a troll!"

I cringed. She said it. Ava couldn't hold back the tears anymore and fled back through the door and up the stairs to the second floor. Perfect. I had to get her out of here before she said anything else.

Ty looked crestfallen. No doubt he'd never been called a troll before. "I'm sorry," he said. "I didn't mean to cause trouble."

Rae still looked shocked, like she couldn't process what had transpired. "Stay here," I told her. "I'll get Ava and then we're out of here."

Ty started to say something else but I raced back into the house and up the stairs. I tried the first door and came across two people who did not seem happy about being interrupted. "Oops, wrong room." I shut the door louder than intended as I turned back to the hallway.

"Most people looking for a bedroom have another person with them. Trying something kinky, or are you looking for someone?" Jay Ashland stood against the wall where a line formed outside what must be the bathroom. He was the last person I'd expect to see at a jock's party.

"No, I, I'm looking for Ava. Have you seen her?"

He jerked his thumb in front of them. "Yeah, she cut in line and ran in there. She looked pretty upset. Everything okay?"

"Not even close." I jumped in front of the line and ignored the grumbling of the people in line. "Ava, open up. We have to go." I pounded on the door.

Ava's muffled voice came through the door. "I'm not going anywhere with you."

Several girls in line started whispering. This was sure to be gossip-worthy at school tomorrow.

I knocked more loudly. "Please, A. I'll explain everything."

Jay came over and touched my arm. "Can I help?"

"Sure. I'm not getting anywhere."

I'd thought he meant he would try talking to her, but instead he backed up and headed at the door.

"Jay, wait, I didn't mean—"

Right as he reached the door, Ava opened it. He flew into her and sent them both crashing to the bathroom floor. Luckily, Ava landed on her butt rather than her head and Jay landed on top of her. One of the girls who had been whispering behind me stepped close to me and had her cell phone raised. This little episode couldn't go viral.

I jumped inside the bathroom and slammed the door in the girl's face. After locking it, I offered my hand to Jay and helped pull him off the floor.

"Are you guys okay?" I tried to help Ava, but she ignored my hand and got up on her own.

Ava laughed through her tears. "I'm just great. You know, aside from the fact that this is the worst day of my life. You're such a traitor."

At least she hadn't called me a troll.

Jay looked at me quizzically with his big brown eyes. I didn't want to tell him about what happened. I didn't want him to think badly of me.

Her tone was harsh and accusatory. "You like Ty."

I didn't know what to say. I mean, I did like him, but how do you tell your best friend that you like her crush?

Jay exhaled like he was relieved. "Obviously, but that's no big deal. She's liked him for forever."

Ava looked like someone slapped her in the face.

I wanted to kill Jay. He had no idea how much worse he just made things.

Ava took a deep breath. "I'm out of here. I'll find my own ride." She stormed toward the door, and I grabbed her arm to stop her.

Jay reached for me. "What? Did I say something wrong?"

It came out of nowhere.

The swirling black funnel appeared in the middle of the bathroom and engulfed all three of us.

9

We appeared in a small chamber room in the Queen's quarters. I reached down to find that Rae's small flask had made the trip and was in my tunic pocket. Rolph, scepter in hand, stared in horror at us. "Darling, the Queen doesn't even know you left. She thinks you're out looking for Muriel. How on Earth am I supposed to explain ... this ..." He eyed Jay. "... this peasant?"

Jay stared from the castle room around us to Rolph. "What ... where ... did he just call me a peasant?"

"Rolph! Rolph! Where are you?" The Queen's voice called from a nearby room.

Rolph dropped the scepter into a chair. He spoke in a hushed whisper. "She woke up earlier than usual. You all have to get out of here now. Go!" He shooed us away with his hand. "And Bree, you need to keep this ... person ... out of sight, or the Queen will have my head."

"Coming, your Majesty," Rolph called in a loud voice.

I tugged on their sleeves. "Let's go." We had to get into the forest quickly or we'd be seen by someone for sure. We couldn't even take Majestic since we'd have to stay off the paths.

As we ran into the thick foliage, I attempted to explain Liralelle to Jay. He wasn't nearly as receptive to the idea as Ava had been.

"This isn't possible. Someone must have put something in my drink." Jay smacked himself in the face, which I had wanted to do when we were back in the bathroom. He looked around and found himself still surrounded by leafy green trees with bright flowers. "This isn't possible," he repeated.

"Oh, it's possible," Ava said. She wouldn't look at me as she swatted away a low-hanging tree branch. "I'm still mad at you, you know."

I moved in front of them to help clear some sort of path with my sword. I whacked at the thicket to make it easier to pass through. "A, you have to believe me, I never in a million years thought he would notice me."

Ava scoffed. "Well, he's definitely noticed you, but that's not the point. The point is that you knew I liked Ty, but you never once told me that you liked him too."

Jay stopped in his tracks, staring at me. "Wait, how do you have a sword? Why are you dressed like that—did you change clothes or have you been like that?" Then he shook his head. "This is ridiculous. And how can you both be arguing over a guy when we've taken a ride on some crazy train? Am I the only one here who thinks this is nuts?"

Ava stepped around him and patted him on the shoulder as she went by. "Oh, I've been here before. Don't worry."

"Seriously? You've been *here*?" He looked kind of cute with his mouth hanging open.

"Well, yeah, that tornado thing brings us back and forth." She glared and stomped ahead like she knew where she was going. "I'm still helping with Muriel, but only because it's the right thing to do. After that, we're through—"

Ava tripped and fell on her face.

It took me a second to realize that it wasn't a tree limb that she tripped over. It was an actual limb.

"Oh, good God," Jay gasped. "Is that a leg?"

Fear clamped my throat shut.

"What the hell kind of place is this?" Jay sounded horrified.

"L-leg?" Ava craned her neck to see what she tripped over and a strangled cry escaped her lips.

"Shhhh! Be quiet—we don't know who else is here." I scanned the surrounding trees but heard nothing. Just a few birds tweeting like it was the most beautiful day ever.

The body was face down with the head turned to the side, but my stomach tightened into knots. I'd heard about the missing teenage girls from the village, but this one hadn't been missing last time I was here.

Her face was obscured by the matted hair that fell across her cheek. The luster was gone, but it was still black as night. Torn fishnets covered her legs, and her hand reached out on one side, chipped red nails still clutching at an unseen assailant.

I knew it wouldn't matter, but I had to try anyway. I knelt down and touched her arm. "Snow?" I nudged her arm a little harder. It wasn't rigid yet, so whatever happened hadn't been long ago.

I brushed the hair back from her face, and her black-rimmed eyes stared straight ahead. The saddest part was she didn't have the shocked, surprised look I'd seen on many of the witches and other assorted creatures I'd killed. She looked resigned, almost like she expected that being killed was something that would happen to her someday. The look wasn't too different than when I'd seen her last in the bar—hopeless.

"She's dead." Ava huddled on the ground with her legs tucked under her. She rocked back and forth.

I closed Snow's eyes. "I'm sorry," I said to her, though I didn't know why. Something was odd about her skin. It was whiter than it should be, even for a dead person, even for someone as pale as Snow was to begin with. I pulled her hair back further and noticed the mark on her neck.

"Oh crap." Jay leaned over me and covered his hand with his mouth. "There are vampires here?"

"No, no vampires." The mark wasn't made from teeth. It didn't even look like a slash. The cut was clean and straight. The end result was the same as a vampire though— she'd been drained entirely of blood.

Ava whimpered. "I changed my mind about helping. I want to go home."

"I want to go home too but I can't yet. I promise to get you home as soon as possible." I stood up and looked around. "We can't leave her like this. Jay, will you help me?"

He grimaced but nodded. We turned her over. I grabbed Snow's ankles and he hoisted her under the shoulders. There was a small clearing to our left, and we carried her into it. I figured that Her Highness could send people for a proper burial when we got back, but this would have to do for now. Ava sobbed silently but picked flowers from the trees and sprinkled them on top of Snow's body. I placed a few pink ones in her hair, and they shimmered against the jet black tresses. Such a waste.

"Thanks, guys. We need to go. Muriel can't be far from here, and we need to find her."

Ava choked back more tears. "I was afraid you were going to say that."

"Who's Muriel? And why are we going after her? Aren't there police for that?"

Ava glanced grudgingly in my direction. "She is the police."

Jay's mouth dropped open again. We hadn't had time to give him the full story before, but it's not like this was a great time to catch him up to speed. For all I knew, we were being watched. We went back toward the spot where Ava had tripped. I stole a final glance at Snow before we moved into the trees. Dappled sunlight shone on her pale arms crossed in front of her. The strewn flowers made her look like a sleeping angel. Maybe she'd finally be at peace.

I faced ahead and moved as quickly as I could, slicing my sword through the tangled brush. Every time I heard the snap of a branch, I'd turn back to see Ava shrug sheepishly. "Sorry, it's just me," she whispered.

Jay stayed near her side and right behind me. Every once in

awhile he'd give his opinion in a low voice. "This place is awful. Dead girls in forests, evil witches. Fairyland is worse than Detroit."

"Did you not read any Grimm's fairytales?" Ava whispered back. "Hello, witches killing children all over the place. It wasn't until Disney took over that everything became all innocent and magical."

"Shhh. Both of you, just shhhh." A twig snapped in the distance, and I knew it wasn't Ava this time. I put my arm out to stop them and surveyed the woods. The light had grown dimmer, so it had to be late afternoon. Jay and Ava stood still behind me with baited breath.

I stepped toward the trees where the sound came from. Maybe it was just an animal, hopefully a small one at that.

"AAAAARG!" The battle cry preceded the raised sword of someone who crashed through the trees toward us.

Ava, who'd crouched into a kickboxing pose, ran behind me and ducked. Jay, who to my knowledge had only ever been armed with a weapon of the trumpet variety, put his arm across me as if he could protect me from a sword with his bare skin. It was dorky but sweet.

"Halt!" I cried. "Unless you are prepared to die. I am Bree, witch slayer of Liralelle." I stepped in front of Jay's arm and readied my sword.

The sword-wielding attacker broke through the last trees, but he was already lowering their sword. "Bree? Is that you?"

"Evan!" The delight in Ava's voice was unmistakable.

Jay took in Evan's baggy green pants and open shirt with a ruffled collar. "You know this guy? What, do you guys come here instead of study hall after Lit class?"

Evan sheathed his sword and bowed low. "Ladies, my mistake." He reached out and grabbed Jay's hand to shake it. "I'm Evan."

Jay extracted his hand from Evan's. "Clearly. I'm Jay."

"Prince Evan, to be exact," Ava added.

"Of course he is." Jay didn't seem happy about the new arrival.

Evan pulled us into a huddle. "Sorry to surprise you, but Muriel's been this way.

I remembered his vow to find her, but I no longer cared about the competition. In fact, I welcomed it. I told him about Snow.

Evan's face darkened. "I spotted Muriel around here earlier, but lost track of her. It's my fault Snow's dead."

"No, it's my fault for leaving when I should have tracked her down immediately," I said.

Jay looked between us. "Not to break up the guilt fest, but it seems like it's actually Muriel's fault, and I don't even know who the hell she is."

I didn't need anyone to make me feel better. I'd feel better once Muriel was dead. "Where did you last see her?"

Evan frowned. "I lost track of her right around here. It's like she just disappeared."

Horace had used almost the same words to describe her, something about Muriel disappearing into the night. Speaking of night, the sun hung heavy on the horizon. Light slipped away with each passing minute, and a chill permeated the air.

"Are we near any villages?" I asked. I'd never been out this far into the surrounding woods and had no clue how far we'd come.

"Yeah, like one with a nice hotel and open buffet?" Ava asked hopefully.

Evan looked uncertain. "I've trekked these woods for years, and as far as I know, this forest stretches on for hundreds of miles with nothing in between."

"Perfect. So, just to clarify, we don't know where we're going or what to do next? Am I following along correctly?" Jay asked. "Oh wait, I have GPS on my phone."

He pulled his phone from his sweatshirt and punched the buttons to no avail.

Ava patted him on the arm like a small child. "There's no wi-fi in Liralelle, sweetie."

Jay let a string of expletives fly into the dusk.

Evan studied the sky. "Well, we're losing light and it won't do any good to wander aimlessly. We should camp here and try to find her trail again in the morning."

Ava shuddered. "Camp out here? In the dark?"

Evan laughed. "Don't worry. It's what I do all the time. I have my sleeping roll, but you can use it."

Ava's eyes lit up. "Sure, or, you know, we could share or something."

Jay leaned over. "Is it me or is he freakishly good-looking?"

I acted surprised. "I hadn't noticed. Maybe a little, I guess."

Jay shrugged and started pulling branches from the trees.

"What are you doing?" I asked.

He twined the branches together and laid them together under the tree. "I believe the man said we were camping. I'm making us a bed." He scooped up handfuls of leaves and scattered them on the makeshift bed.

He'd said us, but did he mean the two of us, or all of us. It certainly didn't look like a bed big enough for four.

"Brilliant," said Evan. "We'll stick together, but since Bree and I have the weapons, I'll watch over Ava, and Bree can guard you."

Ava practically swooned. I knew what she was thinking. She had her very own prince for the night. She helped him lay out his sleeping roll and thin blanket and was probably already imagining them snuggling under it.

I watched Jay twine some leaves into a makeshift blanket. "Where did you learn to do that?"

"My Dad used to take me camping a lot on the weekends. Taught me a lot of survival stuff that I thought I'd never need. Guess he'd be proud."

"Don't you go with him anymore?"

Jay's eyes darkened as he worked the leaves together. "No, he died."

"I'm so sorry. My dad's dead too."

Jay smiled at me. "Yeah, I know."

I watched his fingers move steadily and surely over the branches. I wasn't used to someone else taking care of me. I'd always been the one taking care of everyone else. It was nice. Weird, but nice.

"I'll start the fire," Evan said. "It'll have to be a small one, just enough to cook. We don't want to attract attention."

Ava collected twigs and arranged them where Evan instructed. He and Jay had gone to break off some bigger pieces and find some food. "You'd make a great Girl Scout," I remarked.

She beamed. "Thanks." It was like she'd forgotten the whole reason we were in the woods was because of a maniacal witch.

I brought over more dry twigs and dumped them on the pile. "I'm just making the best of a bad situation," Ava said, as though she'd read my mind. "Plus, Evan makes me feel safe. No offense, I'm sure you're really great with your sword, but he makes me feel like I can't get hurt."

I'd just been thinking the same thing about Jay. "I get it."

Ava stood and brushed the dirt from her hands. "Also, I want you to know that I forgive you ... for Ty. Life is too short to stay mad at your best friend."

She left unsaid that our life might be much shorter than most given our current circumstances. I hugged her. "Ava, I'm so sorry I never told you I liked Ty. I never, ever would have gone out with him though. I swear. You're way too important to me."

Ava hugged me back. "Just keep your hands off Evan, okay?"

I laughed. "Done."

She twirled a blond curl. "So, is it bad that despite all the crap going on, I'm worried we're going to miss practice and that I'll lose my spot in the show?"

I thought of Adrian and how fast he'd give Catelyn the lead if I missed again. How fast my resume for Juilliard could self-destruct. "No, it's not bad. It's normal. We're just dealing with very abnormal stuff right now."

Ava sighed. "Yeah, tell me about it. Anyway, going back to the boy thing a sec, Jay seems like a cool guy. Anything going on there?"

Heat flushed my cheeks and I was grateful that the sun had faded in the sky. "Maybe. Not sure yet, but I'll keep you posted." The twilight cast shadows across her face. "So, what's going on at home, A? I've been worried about you."

Ava stared out into the woods before looking back at me. "Let's see. Dad's still cheating, Mom's still drinking, and my brother's still a dickhead, so ... yeah, that about covers it."

"I'm so sorry." I didn't know what else to say. My dad might be dead, but my mom was amazing, and my brother was the coolest kid ever. I couldn't imagine what it would be like if my entire family sucked.

She said it so low, I almost didn't hear her. "I'd rather stay here in Liralelle ... except for the witch."

"Okay, ladies, here we go." Evan appeared from the trees carrying several large logs. He also had a small bag hanging around his waist.

Jay followed with an armful of his own logs.

"What's for dinner?" Ava asked.

Jay met my eyes and I knew that the food in Evan's bag wasn't a nice, plump turkey.

"Ugh. I can't even believe I'm eating this." Ava gagged between bites. We sat close together, huddled around the fire. It crackled, giving off warmth and light within the darkness of the forest.

Jay chewed a minute. "It kind of tastes like chicken."

"It's just a squirrel. They're good...I eat them all the time," said Evan, a trace of defensiveness in his voice.

Trekking through the forest had worked up my appetite and I was famished. I didn't care if I was eating a huge rat. I tore into my piece.

Jay laughed. "I like a girl who's into more than salad."

I blushed in the dark and rushed to change the subject. "So, what's your story, Evan? Why do you stick to the woods so much? Shouldn't princes be living in a castle?"

Ava forgot the chewy substance in her mouth and waited for his response.

He tossed a bone aside. "Not me. My parents have pretty much kept me hidden my whole life. They said it wasn't safe for me in Liralelle but wouldn't say why." Evan took a swig of water from his tin cup and passed it to Ava. "Once I got old enough to be on my own, my dad taught me how to live in the woods, just in case. But it suited me, so I've done it more and more." He spread his arms wide. "I love it out here. And as soon as it's safe for me to come out of hiding, they want me to marry Ms. Crazy Pants, so I'm good with the trees … for now."

Ava hung on every word. "But can't the Queen help you?"

"Don't know. I've never met her." Evan peered at me over the fire. "We live on the opposite side of the Kingdom and I'm told she doesn't venture out much past her gates. Anyway, I overheard my parents one night when they were out in the garden. They spoke about the village girls disappearing, and then mentioned Muriel's name." He tossed the last of his bones into the fire and a small spark flew up. "I decided I was going to find Muriel myself."

I pondered his words but couldn't make sense of it. "But there are other princes out there who aren't hiding. They're marrying princesses … princesses without mental health issues." I would know —I'd provided a sort of assassin/matchmaking service for several years.

Evan chuckled. "I know. I heard about Hubert proposing to Rapzy. The guy's a total dork. He's lucky she's dumb as a brick, or she'd wonder how he ever managed to defeat a witch. Now he can climb her long hair for eternity."

Jay choked on his water. "I'm sorry. Rapzy as in, like, Rapunzel?"

My mind churned as I tried to figure something out. "Yes, Rapzy is what the town folk call her, sort of like "ditzy" because she was always tripping over her hair—before she got captured. Anyway, that's not the point." I looked back at Evan. "Why are you not safe and they are?"

Ava cleared her throat. "You did say that he's not like any other Prince in Liralelle, right?"

Jay turned toward me. "You said that?"

Why did everything I say come back to haunt me? "I just meant that I've never seen any who were, um, strong enough to take on a witch themselves. That's part of why I'm needed here."

Jay didn't look convinced. "But he clearly is, so why wouldn't the Queen want to use him rather than go through the trouble of bringing you all the way here?"

He was right. Her Highness had an able-bodied—no, more like super awesome-bodied guy at her disposal—yet she sent for me instead. Why? I frowned. "Maybe she doesn't know you exist ... if you've been hidden by your parents for some reason."

Ava yawned loudly, dramatically even. "This is super interesting, but I'm exhausted and think we should try to get some sleep."

Evan jumped to his feet. "Yes, you must be exhausted. I'll ready your sleeping roll and will take first watch." He pulled his sword from his sheath.

Ava's face fell in disappointment, her hopes of snuggling with Evan likely fading by the moment. I had to make up for what happened with Ty earlier.

"No, I'll take first watch. I'm not even tired," I lied.

Jay stretched his arms over his head. "I'll keep you company."

Ava flashed me a bright smile and walked the short distance to the trees where the sleeping roll was laid out. She hopped into it, with no trace of fatigue that I could see, then patted the spot next to her.

Evan hesitated, but placed his sword back in place and joined her. Evan held up three fingers. "Get me up in three hours. And put the fire out before too long."

I saluted him. "Got it, Prince."

I threw a bit of twig into the fire and watched the small spark. I'd hate to extinguish it because the light was as comforting as the warmth. The chilled night air blew against my back and I shivered.

Jay scooted over closer to me. "Here, you can wear this." He began to unzip his hoodie.

I instinctively put my hand on his arm. "Careful." I gestured at the zipper.

He raised an eyebrow at me. "Yeah, I hear zipper deaths are climbing the list of silent killers, right behind heart disease."

"Sorry, zippers freak me out ... my finger got stuck in one when I was five."

I could tell he was trying not to laugh as he continued unzipping, but then a look of shock overcame his face and his hand shook. "Oh god, oh god." His finger looked stuck.

I jumped to my feet. "What is it?"

He tore off the hoodie in one smooth motion and chuckled. "Just kidding. Here."

I smacked him with my hand. "You're mocking my fear. Jerk."

Jay shrugged. "Excuse my language, but we're in a totally fucked up place, and you're worrying about death by zipper. Yes, I'm mocking you ... but in a nice way."

"Whatever." I pushed the sweatshirt away. "Anyway, you only have a t-shirt on underneath. You'll be cold."

He smiled. "Well, we could share it." He placed one arm of the sweatshirt around me and pulled me closer to him.

Our hands touched briefly as I reached to hold on to the soft material, and a warm, tingly feeling coursed through me. "Thanks."

We sat in silence in front of the crackling flames. Though Ava and Evan lay about twenty feet away, Ava's soft chattering floated toward us and I wondered how Evan would be able to get any sleep. It's not like I was going to reprimand her, because I didn't want to move an inch. Jay's leg pressed against my own and I liked the feel of him against me.

I brushed a piece of stray hair from my face as I stared into the fire. "Thanks, by the way, for helping with Snow back there."

"Sure, it's what anyone would do. Well, anyone transported to an alternate reality populated by demented fairytale characters."

I nudged my leg against his. "Glad you've finally come to terms with all this."

He nudged back and an electric feeling went up my leg. "What I've come to terms with is the fact that I might be having a psychotic episode. I'm reserving further judgment until later."

"Fair enough. So, let's talk about non-psychotic stuff. How long have you wanted to go to Juilliard?"

He scratched his head. "Let's see. Since I was about nine and discovered a school existed where you could consume music day and night. It seemed like heaven to me at the time. Still does. You?"

"I have a picture of me in my first tutu when I was six. I got it as a birthday present, and my mom thought I looked so cute in it that she signed me up for lessons. I've been hooked ever since."

We talked more about our plans and career goals, but it was hard to sort out my thoughts with his body so close to mine. The warmth of him was unsettling, and I wanted to get closer, although it wasn't possible to do that without getting in his lap. Plus, he already thought I liked Ty *and* Evan, and I didn't want him to think I was serial boy stalker.

I stole a glance at him. The fire lit up his profile and he turned toward me before I could look away.

"Hey," he said. His eyes held a warm glow from the flickering flames, as he stared into mine.

"Hey." I couldn't look away.

Jay moved his face closer to mine. His lips were inches away, and they looked soft and inviting. I wanted nothing more in that moment than for him to kiss me.

Ava's squeal pierced the darkness.

I jumped up and pulled my sword in one quick movement.

Jay and I ran over as Evan leapt from the ground, waving his arms around. Ava ran in circles like she was doing some kind of weird rain dance.

"What the—?" Jay asked.

"Something crawled on me. It felt slimy and gross. What if it's still on me?" She shrieked again.

I sighed. "Please stop shrieking. You'll give us away."

Ave immediately clamped a hand over her mouth.

"It's too dark to see over here. Come by the fire and I'll check you." Ava stopped turning in circles and we moved closer to the fire, which was now little more than glowing logs.

Evan bent over, hands on his knees. "She gave me a heart attack. I thought Muriel was here or something."

Ava began to cry. "I'm so sorry. The scream was an involuntary response—I hate bugs with a passion."

Jay and I inspected the back of her and turned her around. Ava flapped her shirt to make sure nothing was crawling underneath. I patted her shoulder. "I think whatever it was is gone now. You're okay."

Evan exhaled. "There are a fair amount of woodland critters but they're harmless—I swear." He peered into the trees. "And I don't hear anything so I think the screams went undetected, which is good." He gently touched Ava's arm. "Come, you need some sleep. Maybe we can get back to ... what's that word you used."

Ava let a small smile escape. "Oh, when I let you put your arm around me? That's called cuddling."

"Cuddling," Evan repeated. "I've never done that before and it's rather pleasant. May we cuddle some more?"

"We may." Ava led him by the hand back to their sleeping area. She inspected the ground before laying down. "And I promise to do my best not to scream again."

I shook my head. "Enjoy the cuddling, you two. Night."

"Night, B," said Ava.

I watched in the dark as Evan carefully laid his arm across Ava, like he was afraid he would break her. She placed her hand on his arm and snuggled against him.

I suppressed a smile, as Jay and I headed back to the fire.

"I know I've said this more than once today, but—unbelievable," he whispered into my ear.

The fire had dwindled down to little more than embers, and Jay helped me kicked dirt onto the remnants.

We were thrust into inky blackness, as the thick forest blocked out most of the moonlight. I instinctively reached for Jay's arm. Though I was used to fending for myself, it was nice to have someone by my side.

He wrapped his arm through mine. "Ready for bed?"

"I can't. I'm still on watch."

Jay led me to his makeshift mattress. "We won't sleep; we'll just rest. I know you need it."

We lay down, and Jay covered us with the hoodie and the blanket of leaves he'd made earlier. I leaned my head against his shoulder and stared up at the sky. A few lone stars were visible between the cover of the trees. The silence coming from nearby told me that Ava's cuddling lesson must be going well. Jay's fingers brushed mine, and I wound my hand through his. If it weren't for the fact that I was hunting a murderous witch and trying to get back home to my brother, I would let myself feel happy.

Thoughts of Jay, my mom, and my brother swirled around in my head. The stars above blinked and twinkled, ignorant of my despair. The rhythmic breathing next to me told me that Jay had fallen asleep, his hand still twisted in mine. I tried to fight it for as long as I could, but in the end, I failed. I did the unthinkable.

I fell asleep.

10

I vomited onto the ground, my insides twisted in a violent knot. It wasn't possible. Evan said he'd slept with his arm around her almost the entire night. I circled back to where Evan hunched over the empty sleeping roll.

He punched the ground. "I betrayed her," he choked.

I wiped my mouth on my sleeve. "Tell me again what happened." My stomach heaved again.

Evan ran his hand through his unkempt hair. "I had my arm around her when dawn broke. I thought we'd made it safely through the night ... I must have drifted off. What have I done?"

"Then what?" My stomach turned again. Jay circled around an area in the woods near the sleeping roll.

"I ... I woke ... and she was just gone. I thought maybe she'd gone into the woods to ... you know. But I couldn't find her anywhere. That's when I started calling out her name and you guys woke up."

I knew Ava would never have gone into the woods, not even to pee, without having me go with her. And if someone had taken her, why hadn't she screamed out or made a sound? I was a light sleeper and would have heard her. Tears leaked out of my eyes. Thoughts of Snow's blood-drained body caused a fresh wave of nausea. We didn't have much time to find her, or she'd be the next dead body in the woods.

"Did you find anything?" I asked Jay.

Jay didn't respond and I noticed he was bent over something on the ground. Oh God. I ran toward him, and he looked up with an expression of shock on his face.

He looked almost as pale as Snow had been.

"What, what is it?" I pushed through a branch to where he hunched down.

He held up one of Ava's bright green sneakers.

Sobs tore from my throat. How could I have let this happen? Ava was the last person who deserved this. She deserved sunshine and rainbows. Jay came over and put his arm around my shoulder. I cried even harder.

"Okay, we're not going to lose her," Evan said. He placed his hands on both my shoulders, looking me dead-on. "You're Bree, warrior of Liralelle."

I wiped my nose with my sleeve. I wasn't a warrior; I wasn't even a good friend. I sniffled. "How do we save her?"

"The shoe is the only clue we have, but at least it's something. We'll head in the direction where Jay found the shoe until we find her. We've got to move quickly though."

He didn't need to tell me that last part, but it got me motivated to do something other than cry. I secured my sword, and Jay grabbed his hoodie and we were off. We trailed behind Evan, who knew more about tracking than I did. He searched for broken twigs and breaks in the dense foliage where someone could have passed through, while I scanned the forest for possible clues.

"I don't get it," Evan muttered. "There should be some sign that someone came through here somewhere. It's like she just disappeared."

Chills ran through me. That's how everyone described Muriel. I didn't want to believe that she really had Ava, but it didn't look like there was another answer.

"Keep going," I said.

Jay put a reassuring hand on my arm. "We'll find her."

He sounded so sure that I almost believed him. I nodded and kept going.

The sun, having risen higher in the sky, warmed the air. The fragrance from the flowering trees wafted over me, but now smelled sickly sweet instead of lush and vibrant. The twigs pulled as I walked through, and my arms were covered with small scratches. It seemed like we'd been walking forever when we reached a small creek. Jay and Evan slurped up the fresh water. I drank a little, but my stomach remained in knots, which made it difficult. I sank on my knees by the creek bed, my fingers pushing into the soft ground.

Jay came behind me and rubbed my shoulders. "You need water, Bree. It'll give you strength."

Something about his voice grounded me. He was right. I had to stay strong for Ava. I was me, no matter which world I was in, and if I could fight for a bunch of random princesses, I could fight for my best friend. I leaned over, washed my hands, and drank deeply from the cool water. After splashing more water on my face and neck, I sat back on my heels and looked around. There was a small rise on the other side of the creek, and beyond it, what looked like a narrow trail.

"Look!" I jumped up.

Evan looked up and down the length of the creek. "I don't see a place to cross, so we'll just have to go through."

Evan filled his water container, and I remembered Rae's flask and filled that as well. The creek wasn't too deep, about knee height in the middle, as we waded across. A fish jumped out of the water by me, and I almost screamed. The only sound, aside from the soft splashing of water as we trudged through, was the occasional call of a bird. Maybe it was the circumstances, but the bird's sounds seemed less like singing and more like a warning.

We climbed up the small hill on the other side of the creek and came to the narrow trail. And the word trail was an overstatement—it was barely more than a foot across of well-worn, trampled grass. It stretched out as far as we could see in both directions.

"Which way?" Jay asked.

Evan looked left, where the trail veered uphill, away from the creek. "Left. Hopefully we can see better from higher up."

We were able to move faster on the trail, without having to fight the trees for every step. The only problem with going toward higher ground is that it meant constantly walking uphill. The sun was directly overhead now, and despite the cover of trees, sweat beaded on my face and body. My thighs burned by the time we were halfway up the hill. Horses would have made this so much easier, and I wished Majestic were with me. After what seemed like an eternity, we reached the top of the hill and stopped. Jay panted beside me.

The good news was that the trail grew slightly wider here. The bad news was that the only thing visible ahead was more trail. It dawned on me that if we didn't find our way out of here, we might be in just as much danger from being lost as from Muriel.

I kicked at the dirt. "This sucks."

Even Jay couldn't find an encouraging comment.

Evan swallowed hard. "Guess we keep going this way and hope for the best."

We walked onward, and after another hour or so, the trail dipped downward again. I thought of how quiet we were. Ava's constant chatter was noticeably absent.

Evan waved his arms up ahead. I caught up to him and looked where he pointed downhill. A small cottage was tucked away in the trees, barely visible from the trail. My heart beat faster. Maybe we'd finally found Muriel's place. Maybe Ava was there. I urged Jay to move faster.

The house was only several hundred feet away. Evan and I pulled our swords. We moved as quietly and quickly as possible. I told Jay to stay behind me in case we'd already been spotted. I don't know how I could protect him if I couldn't protect Ava, but I had to try. I couldn't bear losing someone else I cared about.

We'd only made it about fifty feet when I heard a noise behind me. I whipped around and stared at the trail behind us. The sound grew louder and I realized it was the gallop of a horse. Evan pulled us back into the trees, but the horse broke into view before I was hidden. Majestic.

I stopped, confused. Riding Majestic was the Queen herself. Another horse followed, with a frantic-looking Rolph astride it.

"Rolph!" I yelled before I could stop myself.

Evan and Jay ran out beside me.

Her Highness stopped in front of me, staring first at Jay and then at Evan.

"Thank goodness you're okay," Rolph said, breathless as he stopped behind the Queen.

"Your Majesty, Ava, my friend, has been taken by Muriel," I stammered. "We think she might be down there." I pointed down the trail.

The Queen's eyes widened as she took in the cottage. "Muriel. Finally."

She reached to her side, and I thought she was going to pull out a sword, but instead, she pulled out her scepter. Her eyes went back to Evan before she addressed me. "Bree, you've found her. Good work."

"Yes, but we must hurry, she has Ava." We needed to move.

"Rolph, her payment."

Rolph nudged his horse toward me and handed me the hugest bag of gold I'd ever seen. I didn't understand. I hadn't killed Muriel yet, and I definitely hadn't saved my best friend.

He thrust the bag into my hand. "Trust me, you've earned this, my dear. Be safe."

"Yes, you certainly have." Her Highness smiled at me. "You've led me to the worst witch this land has ever seen, and I'll take it from here." She raised the scepter. "I couldn't bear for anything to happen to you, Bree. I hereby release you from your commendable service."

She pointed the scepter at me and began chanting the spell to send me home.

"No! I need to get Ava first," I yelled.

Her Highness ignored me and completed the chant. I tried to run for the cottage, but the black funnel veered at me. There was no way I'd be able to outrun it. Jay called out behind me. I stopped short, skidding on the path. I couldn't leave Jay here either. The funnel pulled up large twigs and dirt from the path as it headed my way. I could barely make out Jay's form on the other side as he ran toward me.

Pebbles and dust pelted my face, and I threw up my arm to shield myself. Tears streamed down my face as the tunnel bore down. I had failed—failed Ava, failed my murdered family, failed myself. Jay dove into the funnel as it engulfed me. The last thing I felt was his body slamming into mine.

My cheek pressed against the cold, grimy tile floor. Jay groaned on top of me.

I wanted to scream for Her Highness to take me back, not that she'd hear me. The funnel cloud was long gone, and I had no way back to Liralelle. I reached for Jay in the inky darkness. "Are you okay?"

"I think so, but only because you broke my fall." He put a hand to my tear-stained cheek. "I'm more worried about you."

"Physically, I'm fine. Otherwise, not so much." I let Jay help me to my feet and the gold pieces shifted in my pocket. They clinked together and the sound echoed in the small space. I lowered my voice. "I can't believe we're back in Trevor's bathroom."

That was how it worked, of course, with the tornado putting me back the same place it found me, but up until the past week, that place had always been my bedroom.

Jay cracked the bathroom door, and I held my breath when it squeaked. With my luck, Trevor's parents would think that people were breaking into the house and come after us. The whole house was dark and quiet. Only faint light from the moon outside lit up the hallway. Jay put a finger to his lips, and we tiptoed toward the stairs.

The gold lay heavy in my pocket. I'd never gotten so much before, and the weight of it about tipped me over.

Loud, deep snoring came from one of the rooms. It had to be the middle of the night, which might or might not work in our favor. We needed to get out of the house before I could concentrate on how to get back to Ava. We moved past the room as quickly as possible and headed for the stairs. We'd gotten halfway down when I tugged on the back of Jay's shirt.

He paused and then I knew he heard it too. More snoring, but this time coming from downstairs. It came from the direction of the living room, so I motioned toward the kitchen. We'd head out the back door instead. Jay nodded and we crept silently down the remaining stairs. I fought the urge to tear out of the house at full speed, and really hoped they didn't have an alarm system in place.

Something crashed in the living room and I jumped.

Someone muttered in the dark. "Dude, watch it. Trevor will have your balls if you break anything."

"Yeah, yeah." Someone shifted on the couch and the snoring resumed.

We made it to the bottom and jetted toward the kitchen. Beer bottles littered the counters, and the cooler sat in the same part of the kitchen, water now pooled underneath it from the melted ice. The party was definitely over.

"No way," Jay whispered. "It's the *same* night."

"Yeah, told you time works differently there. C'mon, let's get out of here." I needed to find a way to get back to Liralelle.

We slipped out the screen door in the back and hurried down the street. My car still sat on the side of the road, no longer surrounded by the multitude of other cars that had been there earlier. I was so happy to see Kermit that I didn't even care what Jay might think about it.

"Hop in," I said.

I turned on the ignition, and Kermit sputtered to life.

Jay leaned his head back against the seat and ran his hand through his hair. "What now? How do we get back there?"

Tears sprang to my eyes again. "I don't know."

He cranked his head sideways to study me. "What do you mean? I thought you went there all the time."

I shook my head. "Only when I'm summoned. I don't know of any way to get there without being called back."

"Well, no offense, but it didn't sound like she was planning to call you back anytime soon."

"I know. I don't get it. I mean, I get that she wanted Muriel, but I don't understand why she wouldn't let me help Ava."

Jay scratched his head. "She seemed a little preoccupied. Let's just hope that she found Ava ..."

He didn't add "in time," but I knew he thought it. He rushed on, "I mean, if she found Ava and defeated Muriel, then everything will be okay, right? She'll just send Ava back here?"

That was too many ifs for my liking, but I relaxed slightly. I'd led Her Highness right to Muriel, and she had both Evan and Rolph to help her in battle—though I doubted Rolph had anything more lethal than a riding crop on him. Still, their odds were good, and Ava would be rescued ... and returned to Trevor's bathroom. Yikes.

"I guess. I just feel so useless. I wish I knew what was going on. The not knowing is so frustrating." I started driving.

Jay gave me the cross-streets to his house and reached over to squeeze my hand. "At least we have the whole weekend, and don't have to worry about school. Hopefully, we'll hear something in the next few days."

"Yeah." The weekend also meant that I didn't have to worry about Aidan or missing practice. Not that it mattered. Playing the lead part and getting into Juilliard no longer seemed important. Catelyn could have the lead for all I cared. It would be too weird not having Ava there.

It was funny. After Dad died, I threw myself into ballet as if nothing else mattered. I could lose myself in the music for hours without worrying about anybody else. But in the end, I couldn't escape the fact that my friends and family meant everything to me.

I linked my hand through Jay's and drove left-handed. My mom would have disapproved and lectured about safe driving habits, but this was the safest thing I'd done in the last twenty-four hours. After navigating through several subdivisions, we reached his house. I pulled up to the curb and left the motor idling.

Jay didn't move. "I really don't want to let go of you. I'm afraid you could just disappear on me."

I didn't want to let go either as he rubbed my hand with his thumb. "That's always a possibility with me." I looked at our entwined hands and felt suddenly shy. "Maybe you could come over tomorrow? Help me think of a way to get back there."

He smiled at me. "I was already planning on it. But technically, it already is tomorrow, so I thought I'd stop by this afternoon, after we both get some sleep."

Sleep sounded awesome, but I thought of Ava again. She probably wasn't sleeping. You had to be alive to be able to sleep.

"Stop." Jay leaned over. "Stop worrying. I see it in your face. Get some sleep, and I'll see you later." He brushed his lips against mine, and they were warm and comforting. I wanted more. I wanted him to kiss me again so I could forget about everything else for a minute. It would be easy to escape for a while if only he'd touch me again. He didn't.

He pulled slowly away from me, untangled his hand, and climbed out of the car. Before shutting the door, he leaned back down with a serious expression on his face. "Promise you'll be home this afternoon?"

I didn't want to make a promise I wasn't sure I could keep, because it wasn't entirely up to me.

I managed a weak smile. "That's the plan."

MY HOUSE WAS DARK, save for the front porch light, when I got home. My brother had to be sleeping soundly, hopefully dreaming of football or video games. I couldn't wait to see his face. Then, maybe I could try to sleep. I unlocked the front door and snuck inside, slipping my shoes off so as not to be heard on the hardwood floors.

A lamp turned on in the family room next to me. "It's 4am. We need to talk."

Great. I sighed and sank into the chair opposite the couch where Mom sat. It was one of the few times I was jealous of the kids with parents who didn't care where they went or how late they came home. "Sorry, Mom, the party went later than I thought. I'm fine though, you didn't need to wait up."

Mom stood and walked over to me. She brushed the hair back from my face and pulled a small twig from my hair. "Sweetie, I was born at night ... but it wasn't last night."

She tipped my chin back and forth, looking at my face, before taking in the multitude of scratches on my arm. It didn't dawn on me until then just how bad I must look. Trekking through the woods and getting sucked up by a tornado didn't exactly make for a great fashion statement. I hoped she wouldn't notice the bulge of the gold in my pocket. I couldn't tell her what had happened. She'd never believe me, and then I'd have to see a shrink, who would tell her that I'd created a whole fantasy world because I couldn't accept my dad's death.

Whatever story I came up with, it had to be good. She had to believe it.

She took a step back, not taking her eyes off me. "Did someone hurt you?"

Yes, a wicked witch stole my best friend and wants to drain her blood. "No, Mom, I'm fine. I swear."

"So you keep saying." She sat back across from me and folded her hands in her lap. "Unless this party involved rolling around in the woods, I'd say there's something you're not telling me, young lady."

She only pulled out the 'young lady' moniker when she was really upset. I couldn't even remember the last time she'd used it. How the heck could I explain how I looked without alarming her?

Mom cleared her throat. "I was your age too, once, you know. I remember what it's like to be young and impulsive."

I stared at her. Where was she going with this?

"I'm going to go out on a limb here and say that there's a boy involved. Hmm?"

My mouth fell open. No way could she think that my shredded appearance was due to a wild night of forest sex with a boy. But if she did think that ...

I gulped and tried to look guilty. Ballet came naturally to me; acting did not. "Um, well, there is a boy I like."

Mom nodded. "I thought so. I can't believe you've grown up so fast. I feel like just yesterday, you were coloring with me and watching cartoons with Dad ..." She trailed off at the mention of Dad, and we both fell silent.

I couldn't do it. I couldn't let her think those things about me. "Mom, we didn't ... I mean ... nothing happened."

She raised an eyebrow at me and gestured at my hair again.

"Well, okay, something happened, but *that* didn't happen."

Mom exhaled an audible sigh of relief. "Oh, thank the stars. I'm not ready for that. I mean, I don't think you're ready for that."

I laughed. "I think it's safe to say we're both not ready for that. But I do like him." I thought of Jay's kind eyes and warm hands. "He's nice. And smart."

Mom smiled. "That's what drew me to your father. I wish he was here to see how amazing you've become." Her eyes looked far away. "Anyway, I want you to know that you can talk to me about anything. Especially when you feel you are ready, but I hope that's not for a very long time."

She stood and stretched out her arms to give me a hug. I pressed my arm against my pocket to keep the gold coins from jingling as I got up from the chair. She wrapped her arms around me, and I buried my face in her shoulder. She still smelled like the hospital, but it was familiar and that was a good thing. I wished I could tell her how much I was hurting about Ava—Mom thought of Ava like family—and maybe she would know what to do. But it wasn't a normal situation and I didn't see how worrying her would help.

"Okay, now go shower," Mom said.

She didn't need to tell me twice. I started for the stairs.

"And one more thing, young lady."

Here it comes. "Yeah, Mom?"

"You're grounded for the rest of the weekend. You're not going anywhere, got it?"

That was fine with me. The only place I wanted to go was my bed.

CAL SLEPT with his arm curled around a stuffed polar bear. I smiled and pulled the covers up to his chin. He turned over on his side and cracked his eyes. "'Night, night," he murmured sleepily and fell back asleep.

I ruffled his hair and kissed his forehead. "Night, kiddo."

I stripped off my tattered clothes and tucked the bag of gold deep into my closet with the other payments. The coins didn't bring me the joy it usually did after a job. I felt a little sick looking at it, like I had somehow traded Ava for money.

I reached in to turn on the shower and let the water heat up, when I caught sight of myself in the mirror. Holy crap. I'd significantly underestimated how bad it was. My hair, frizzy on a good day, stuck out in bizarre patterns all over my head. Bits of grass and leaves clung to it, and my forehead and cheeks were streaked with dirt. I couldn't believe that Jay had kissed me looking like this. There was nothing about me even remotely attractive at the moment.

I hopped in the shower and let the hot water run over my head. Ty Wilder popped into my head. He wouldn't have wanted to kiss me looking like, that's for sure. It crossed my mind that he'd only acted interested in me after I'd gotten the lead in Sleeping Beauty. Maybe it was less about me and more about his wanting to be seen with the best, no matter who it was. The fact that I'd ever be considered a status symbol was hilarious, but I didn't want that. I wanted a guy who liked me even when I had sticks in my hair.

I put on my favorite cotton sweats and t-shirt, and crawled into bed. My eyes drooped as soon as my head sank into the pillow. Weird images swirled together in that state between waking and dreaming. Rolph gossiping with the stable boy, the Queen sitting in her throne and pointing her scepter at an unseen person, Ava giggling with Prince Evan. I'd find a way to get back to her, no matter what. There had to be way to get myself to Liralelle. Maybe the answer would come in my dreams.

"A*va, you're okay! Oh, thank goodness.*" *I hugged her and stepped back to look around.*

We stood in the middle of a forest in daylight, but the trees crowded us, with their branches poking my skin.

Ava didn't answer. Her eyes looked beyond me.

I checked behind me but didn't see anything. "A, are you okay? Did she hurt you?"

I turned back around.

She was gone.

I spun around, but Ava was nowhere to be seen. The tree branches grew longer and sharper before my eyes. One pierced my shirt, drawing blood from my arm. I pulled away and started to run.

"Ava!" I called out, as I ran. "Ava!"

Only a crow cawed in response. I struggled to get through the trees, and bits of my clothes were ripped off by the hungry branches. Tears streamed down my face, as I fought for every step to find my best friend.

The branches retreated without warning, and a crown was visible in front of me through the trees. I ran toward it, and saw Her Highness, head bowed. Rolph stood near her and he met my eyes as I raced toward them. He only shook his head and lowered his head.

Ava laid on the ground before him, her skin white as snow, a trail of blood from her neck. Her eyes stared up at the sky, seeing nothing.

"No!" I screamed over and over again until my voice grew hoarse.

12

The screaming didn't stop when I woke up, but it wasn't mine. The hair prickled on the back of my neck. I jumped out of bed to the sound of Mom's screams. No. Oh God, please no. My legs shook as I ran down the hallway. She stood in the center of Cal's room, staring at his bed and screaming at the top of her lungs. It was empty. On the floor by his bed was the screen from his window that had to have been pushed in from the outside. Cool morning air blew through the empty space in the window frame.

This wasn't happening. My stomach sank like it was in a free fall. Not Cal. Not my little brother. Again. Flashbacks of my little brother from Liralelle surfaced—his crumpled body on the floor with Muriel standing over him. My knees were shaking so hard but I had to keep it together. I couldn't lose Cal. A strange sense of calm came over me.

My mom sobbed and raced past me. "I'm calling 911. Don't go anywhere."

I walked over to his bed and placed my hand on the spot where he'd been curled around his polar bear hours earlier. The sheets were still warm. The polar bear was nowhere in sight. What were the odds that someone would kidnap my brother on the same day that my best friend disappeared in another land? It didn't make sense. It was too random.

Sirens wailed in the distance. The police would be here in minutes, but I felt in my gut that they wouldn't find anything. They'd do an intensive search, exhaust all kinds of false leads, and ultimately declare it unsolved. I walked to the window and studied it, being careful not to touch it.

My eyes scanned around the frame but there was nothing. I thought a minute. As far as I knew, the only way to Liralelle involved the tornado, but a tornado wouldn't have pushed in a single window screen and it would have appeared inside the room anyway. What if someone could make themselves appear here if they had the right equipment, say a crown and scepter? Like when she dropped me off at the orphanage when I was six-years-old. I suspected Her Highness might have other contacts in this world because of the book deals with the fairytales. But why would anyone want Cal, and why go through the trouble to make it look like a kidnapping?

I searched the room on hands and knees around Cal's bed but didn't find anything. The sirens screamed down our street. Maybe I was wrong. Maybe it was a random kidnapping and I was tampering with everything. My fingers combed the rug by his bed and I peered underneath to see if something had fallen. Nothing. Not even a polar bear.

Police cars screeched to a stop in front of our house, and I pulled my head out from under the bed. A glint of something caught my eye as I stood. A few specks on the edge of his pillowcase. It looked like gold dust. He wasn't an arts and crafts type kid, so I doubted it was glitter. I touched it and it disintegrated in my hand. Though I'd never seen the substance before, it had to be from Liralelle. The anguish in the pit of my stomach hardened into anger. Muriel was not taking my baby brother or my best friend from me. I was going to find a way there. My eyes flew to his bookshelf and fell on the fat book of fairytales that Cal begged me to read night after night. I grabbed the book and ran down the stairs as the officers were racing up.

Mom's voice was hysterical and shrill while showing the police to

Cal's room. More officers pulled up to the house as I reached the living room. I let them in and answered their questions as best I could. Their eyes took in the fairytale book I clutched in my hand. They probably thought it was a grief reaction.

"That one of his favorite books?" an officer asked.

I nodded.

A female officer shook her head. "Crazy ass world."

I slunk to the couch and opened the book like I was trying to find his favorite story. But I wasn't interested in George and the Dragon. My interest was in the copyright page. I scanned the page with my finger and tried not to scoff at the 2020 copyright date. No one had a clue how old these stories were. My eyes found the publisher. I felt stupid for never having checked it out before, but that was when I thought things were cut and dry. Kill the witch, get paid, go to Juilliard.

Maleficent Publishing House, Inc. New York, NY. Figured. New York was more than a hop, skip, and jump from me, and I didn't have a funnel cloud to take me there. Maybe I could reach them by phone. I glanced at the officers hovering around the house. They would find it strange if I insisted I had to call a publisher in the midst of my brother's disappearance. I could call Jay though.

His sleep-filled voice answered on the third ring. "Bree? You okay?"

"My brother's missing."

The sleepiness left his voice. "I'll be right over."

He hung up, and just knowing he was on his way made me feel better. I was so used to taking on so much responsibility—in this world and the other—that it felt good to have someone else around.

I saw there was a voicemail from Rae. She'd probably been freaking out about how Ava and I disappeared from the party and wondered where we went. I had no idea what to tell her. I bet I would soon have voicemails from Ava's mom too. Panic gripped me. How could I not think of that? Ava was missing too, and her mom probably thought she slept at my house. At some point she would wonder why Ava wasn't home yet. It was bad but I hoped she was drinking as much as Ava said and would be sleeping off a hangover. What could I possibly tell her that wouldn't sound completely crazy?

The officers and my mom came back downstairs to join the others. The female officer and another guy asked me some questions on my own in the living room, apparently to rule out my mom as a suspect. Seriously?

I grew more agitated with each question. "Enough. This is seriously messed up. My mom is the best ever and would never hurt Cal."

"I believe you, but sadly, it's most often the case," the female cop told me.

"It's just procedure," the other guy added.

I really wanted to tell him where he could put his procedure. "Well, you're wasting your time." I didn't add that they were wasting their time because he was somewhere they would never find.

The woman spoke in a soothing tone. "We have two guys up there now collecting evidence, dusting for prints. We'll let you know as soon as we find something."

"Some will obviously be mine. Can I see my mom now?"

The woman nodded. "Absolutely, we're all done here."

I walked into the kitchen where Mom stood among the officers, looking lost and confused. She kept picking up and lowering her coffee mug without taking a sip. I rushed over and hugged her, and she leaned down and cried into my hair. After a bit, we sank into chairs at the kitchen table in silence. I usually had a plan for everything but didn't know what to do.

Another hour passed of officers looking around and asking questions before we were told that the two men upstairs would be finished soon and they promised to call with any updates. Then they left.

An eerie, empty quiet filled the house. No pleading by Cal for sugared breakfast cereal, or wheedling to play video games before doing his weekend chores. Guilt racked me. I'd never even gotten to take him for that game of catch in the park. All he'd wanted was to throw the football to me, and I'd let him down.

My weeping morphed into full-fledged sobs. My mom stroked my hair and let me cry into her shirt.

"Shhh. They'll find him, honey. They have too," she said.

That only made me cry harder. No, they wouldn't find him. They couldn't find him, no matter how good they were at their job. He was gone. I had to find a way to get to Liralelle. Two of the people I cared about most in the world were trapped there.

The doorbell rang. Jay. I wiped the snot from my nose, but knew my eyes were swollen and puffy. He'd certainly seen me looking a mess lately. My mom went to the door for me, while I blew my nose into a tissue. I heard his low tone in the entrance, introducing himself to my mom and telling her how sorry he was to hear about Cal.

She brought him into the kitchen.

I looked at him through tear-stained eyes. "Hey."

He walked over without a word and hugged me. I buried my face into his shoulder and tried not to lose it again. I had the weird thought that my mom must think this was the guy I almost had sex with and suppressed the urge to giggle. Rae would say it was a hysterical grief reaction, and that people sometimes laughed at inappropriate times when faced with horrific circumstances. I wondered if her mom could get me some meds, because I could sure use some. I pulled myself away from Jay and offered him coffee.

He nodded, heavy bags under his eyes. I moved around the kitchen pushing buttons on the coffeemaker in a robotic manner. At least making fresh coffee was something I could manage.

Mom struggled to keep herself calm. "I just wish I'd heard something, anything. I didn't hear a sound."

I took the cup from her hand and dumped the cold coffee into the sink. "I know, Mom. Me either."

I'd been in a dead sleep and doubt I'd have heard bombs going off next to my bed, but what happened to Cal was likely a very quiet process. We sat down at the kitchen table, and when the coffee finished percolating, I poured us all a warm cup. When I handed Jay his coffee, he raised a questioning eyebrow at me. He must suspect that Cal's disappearance was out of the ordinary. I shook my head slightly. As much as I might want to unload all of this on Mom, there was no way she could handle it. I'd have to talk to Jay alone.

Mom took a sip this time before setting her cup down. "Who would do something like this? What kind of person takes a child?"

"Somebody very messed up, Mom. Don't worry. I'm getting him back." I set my cup on the table with more force than intended, and coffee sloshed onto the table.

Mom frowned. "You mean the police will get him back. I'm not letting you out of my sight. You're all I have left." Her voice broke on the last word.

"I'm sure the police will find him," Jay said in a calm voice. "And I don't plan to let Bree out of my sight either, if you don't mind."

I'd have to find a way out of here sooner or later but would have to resign myself to staying put for the time being. "Mom, you look exhausted. Why don't you try to rest and I'll answer the phone if the police call?"

She eyed me. "You look like you haven't slept at all."

If she only knew. "I'm fine, Mom. I'll hang out down here with Jay."

As if on cue, the two remaining police officers came downstairs.

"Did you find anything?" Mom asked.

The officers looked at each other. They looked uncomfortable. One of them finally spoke. "No."

"But fingerprints, surely, on the frame?" Mom's voice had risen an octave.

The officer looked around before responding. "No, ma'am, the frame was clean."

Mom looked confused. "But how is that possible?" A look of horror crossed her face. "Oh God, that means they were wearing gloves, right? Like a professional."

The officer shook his head. "No fibers were found either. And the frame doesn't look wiped down. We're not sure what it all means yet."

"I'll tell you what it means. It means my son is missing and somewhere out there right now." Mom's voice grew shrill. "It means you need to go find him and bring him back to me."

"We will do everything possible to make that happen," the officer said. He pulled out a card. "Please call me with any questions, and we'll be in touch."

He was in a tough spot. There was nothing we wanted to hear from him, aside from "Here's Cal, safe and sound." And I knew he wouldn't be able to say that.

Mom sighed after they left. "Well, I can't sleep, but I'm going to go sit in his room a bit—see if there's anything they missed."

I flashed her a weary smile. "M'kay. Love you, Mom."

"Love you too, sweetie."

THE SOUNDS of Mom's crying floated down the stairs. I'd never felt so utterly hopeless and heartbroken.

Jay scooted closer to me at the table and grabbed my hand. "God, I'm so sorry you're going through all this. What do you think happened? I mean, it has to be related to Ava, right?"

I sighed. "I think so. It's too coincidental."

He nodded. "Any thoughts on how to get back there?"

"Not yet, but I need to make a call. Well, two calls actually. Give me a minute."

First, I called Ava's mom and lied. She didn't answer—likely due to still being asleep from a hangover—and it was easier to lie to her voicemail than to her. I said that the party went really late and Ava had slept over but then said how Cal had disappeared. I didn't have to fake the tears and told her that I really needed Ava to stay through the weekend and support me. I hung up, not believing how much pain I felt—if only Ava was curled up asleep in my bed, dreaming of the one cute prince in Liralelle.

Jay rubbed my arm. "At least that gives us two days to find her before her mom officially freaks out."

I couldn't even think about what would happen if we couldn't save her. "Yeah, two days here, or however long that is in Liralelle. If I can get there ... which brings up phone call number two." I told him about the possible link between the company and Liralelle. I pulled up the phone number for the publishing company from their website.

"What are you going to say?" Jay asked.

"I have no idea." I dialed the number. As expected, I got a recording instead of a live person.

You have reached Maleficent Publishing House, Inc. For general inquiries, please push one; to leave a message, push two; for directory assistance, push three; for other assistance, push four.

Since I was sure my needs fell into the "other" category, I went with option four. After a pause and several clicks, a clipped voice appeared on the other end. "Maleficient Publishing, Emily speaking, how may I be of assistance?"

I froze. I had no idea how Emily could be of assistance, unless she could deliver me to Liralelle and that was sure to come out wrong if I tried to explain.

A sharp huff came through the line. "Maleficent Publishing. Anyone there?"

I gulped. "Uh, y-yes, I'm looking for someone who can help me with some issues related to ..."

"Yes?" Her annoyance came through loud and clear.

Here went nothing. "With some issues related to um, Liralelle."

Dead silence.

I spoke louder. "I said I need help with issues related to a place called Liralelle. Can someone there help me? Maybe someone that has worked with a person named, um, Her Highness, regarding the publication of some fairytales?" I sounded like a crazy person.

Jay put his head into his hands.

A long pause ensued. "Who is this?" The annoyance in her voice had changed to suspicion.

That was a great question and I wasn't sure how to answer it. I didn't want to give too much away. "A friend of Her Highness."

A briefer pause came this time. "Hold please."

Classical music poured through the line. I looked at Jay.

"What's up?" he asked.

"I'm on hold. She hasn't hung up though, so that's good."

The music stopped mid-note. A different female voice spoke. "Clarissa speaking. How exactly do you know Her Highness?"

"I ... I've worked for her in Liralelle. My name is Bree. I know about all the fairytales she sends you because I'm the one she hired to kill all those witches in the stories."

Clarissa chuckled. It wasn't a friendly chuckle. "Really? Because you sound like a girl to me, and those stories all involved princes."

Good grief. I didn't have time to give a lecture on the misogynistic nature of fairytales. "Trust me. It's true." I gave a brief account of my mercenary role in Liralelle. "But I need a way to get back to Liralelle because I haven't finished one of the jobs she hired me for."

"Well, good luck with that." Clarrisa's voice was cold and clear. "It's not like we've ever been there. Her Highness comes to us when necessary, but she usually just sends her guard. Wouldn't she come calling for you herself if she needed you?"

That's how it used to work, but I wasn't sure about anything anymore. I thought quickly. "She would if she could, but I think she's in trouble herself. I'd been trying to help her when I accidentally ended up back here. I need to get back there."

"How convenient for her," Clarissa said. "She promised us a new fairytale—the best fairytale we'd ever seen. You'd think royalty could stick to a contract."

What new fairytale was that? I couldn't believe she'd had time for that with Muriel on the loose and girls dying. "Please, I just need to get back there. Can you help me or not?"

"No, I can't help you. But if you see her, tell her that Queen or not, I expect her to meet her deadline—which is still tomorrow. Good bye." A sharp click echoed in my ear.

I lowered the phone. That had been my last shot at getting to my brother and Ava. There was nothing else I could do. I slumped to the floor and cried.

13

J ay pulled the comforter up to my shoulders. The last thing I wanted to do was sleep, but he'd basically carried me up to my bed and insisted that I lay down. He touched my cheek with his finger. "Try to get some rest. I'll be right downstairs on the couch."

I stared at the walls of my room. I'd always felt safe here. The world of Liralelle had been a sometimes dangerous but separate world from mine. Now that the two worlds had blurred together, I didn't feel safe anywhere. My mom must have fallen asleep in Cal's room, because I didn't hear anything.

I drifted off for a bit but woke with a start. Mid-afternoon light spilled through the curtains. I shot straight up in bed and sat very still. Something felt strange in the room. Air currents flowed over my arm yet the window was shut. A fast vibration hummed nearby.

The wall itself looked like it wavered, as the air in front of it undulated and started to glow. Nothing like this had ever happened before. The air slowly changed to a rotating formation. A small funnel appeared that ran from the ceiling to the floor, only it wasn't one of the dark ones that usually came. This one was shimmery gold.

The golden tornado moved toward me but didn't have the fierce winds of the darker one. I wanted to call out to Jay but stopped myself. Ava and Cal were already in peril. I couldn't bring Jay back there and endanger his life too. I wanted him to live and go to Juilliard. I stood up on my bed and dove into the funnel, making a mental apology to Mom. She was going to have a serious meltdown when she realized I was gone too. I prayed that somehow the tunnel would bring me straight to Ava and Cal.

I opened my eyes, but I wasn't in the familiar castle courtyard. In fact, I wasn't anywhere I recognized. The room I'd landed in was dark and small. I'd hoped that the gold color of the tornado meant that Muriel had been defeated and Liralelle was free of evil. That Cal and Ava were together, safe and sound.

My eyes attempted to adjust to the lack of light. A slow, creaking sound came from across the room. I squinted and could just make out a stooped figure moving ever so slightly in the corner. Something glimmered near their head. They reached out and a gas lamp flared to life on a tiny table.

Muriel sat in a wicker rocking chair. She continued rocking, the chair creaking with every movement. The air flew out of me as her watery eyes fixed on me. A crown sat on her head, which was what I'd seen shimmering in the dark. In her lap lay a scepter. They were almost identical to those of Her Highness. Except Muriel's crown had one empty spot where the citrine stone should have been. I felt sick. She'd been the one in the woods with Helga. She had killed her. How she had a crown and scepter in the first place was beyond me. A crooked smile crossed her face. "Bree."

My hand flew to where my sword should be but nothing was there. I was still in my normal clothes. None of the usual things had happened when I was called to Liralelle this time. I backed away from her and surveyed my surroundings.

It appeared to be a small cottage. Likely, the same one I'd seen right before Her Highness sent me away. I quickly scanned the room. A small table was to my right but the wall behind it was solid as was the wall behind me. There was a window on the wall opposite me, but Muriel was in front of it. One door was visible to the left of me. If

I ran really fast, I could probably make it. While I had no idea exactly where it went, I figured anywhere away from Muriel was a good start. My heart pounded in my chest.

"Go on, child." She raised her bony finger toward the door.

Maybe it was a trap. I hesitated a second before deciding I'd risk it. I darted toward the door and flung it open. It led to a small grassy area, and beyond it laid the forest. If I could just get to the trees, I had a chance of hiding from her.

As I stepped outside, Evan raced past me. I'd have thought he was running for his life too, except for the laughter. How could he find this funny?

"I'm going to catch you, Evan."

My heart dropped at the sound of his voice. I turned, and Cal ran toward us, churning his legs to catch up to Evan.

"Cal!" My voice squeaked as I called his name, and he veered toward me and hugged me. I picked him up and squeezed him to me. "Are you okay?"

Cal looked up at me with his big trusting eyes. "Sure. This place is neat. Muriel came to my room inside a gold tornado and brought me here ... how cool is that? She said you'd be here soon." He grabbed my hand. "You said the magic in my fairytale book wasn't real, but it is!"

I still didn't understand why we were here. I swiveled to find Muriel in the doorway, watching us with that crooked smile and those milky eyes. "Where are we? Why did you take Cal?"

Muriel tapped the scepter against the ground. She hobbled out a few steps, using it as a walking stick.

I gripped Cal tighter. "I didn't say to come near me. I said I wanted an explanation."

Evan trotted over to me and placed a hand on my arm. "It's okay. Just listen to her."

Had everyone gone crazy? Cal squirmed until I let him down, but I kept his hand firmly in mine.

"Why don't we go back inside?" Muriel asked. "My legs don't work the way they used to, and the boys can play out here."

"If you think I'm letting Cal out of my sight again, you're crazy.

You're a murderer and a kidnapper and I'm supposed to care about your legs?" I pulled Cal backwards with me.

Muriel sighed. "Very well, we'll do it here." She used the scepter to lower herself in the grass. "I doubt I'll ever be able to get up again though."

If her physical ailments were real, we would have no problem escaping into the woods. I glared at her. "Start talking, and don't forget the part where you tell me where Ava is."

Muriel looked up into the sky and shook her head. "I didn't kill your family, child. I tried to save them. Your parents were too far gone, there was nothing I could do. But your brother ..."

I remembered his little lifeless eyes as his body laid limp on the floor.

"I saw him, Muriel. He was dead."

Muriel nodded slowly. "Yes, he was. But not for as long as your parents. I was trying to bring him back when you came in. That's why I couldn't go after you when you ran away—I didn't have much time. It was difficult but I was able to do it."

Shock and disbelief ran through me. "My brother's alive?"

"'Course. I'm right here, silly," Cal said. He tried to pull away from me to play with Evan again.

Evan gently touched my arm. "Yes, I'm alive. I just found all this out too. That's why you looked familiar the first time I saw you but I was so young then."

I stared at him slack-jawed. Evan was my brother? It still didn't make sense. I thought back to how young I was when I'd found him on the floor. Being young didn't mean my memory was wrong, and Evan's hair and eye color were different than I remembered.

Muriel seemed to read my thoughts. "You think I can bring someone back from the dead, but changing hair color would be a challenge?"

I looked from Evan to Muriel. "But why?"

"To disguise him. He was dead as far as everyone in Liralelle knew. I changed a few of his features, then left him with the folks who agreed to take him in and keep his identity a secret. Good people they are. He was safer that way. It's the same reason I brought Cal here. He was no longer safe in your world."

Evan stared at me. "I never knew what happened to you. You were just gone, and Mom and Dad were gone, and bam—I end up with new parents. No one could tell me anything about you."

Muriel's shoulders sagged. "I didn't know. I thought she'd met the same end as your parents ... until I recently heard about this warrior, Bree. My hunch turned out to be right."

Cal tugged at my arm. "Come on. This is boring. I want to play with my new brother."

Evan smiled at me. "Cal's great. Muriel has a lot more to tell you, so why don't I play tag with him a bit? We'll stay right over here." He hugged me. "I'm so glad we found each other."

I nodded but still didn't know if I could trust what I was hearing. "But stay close. As in, not more than fifty feet away close."

Cal immediately jumped up and tagged Evan's hand. "You're it!" He took off running, then hesitated and asked Evan how far fifty feet was.

My world felt like it had been turned upside down. Things I thought I'd known for sure weren't true. My brother, who I'd seen dead with my own eyes, wasn't dead. Muriel, who I'd seen hovering over his body, hadn't killed him and might not be the most evil witch in existence after all.

Which brought up another question. I turned to face her. "If you didn't kill my family, then who did?"

Her face creased into a frown. "My sister, I'm sad to say. I know her as Gertrude. I believe you know her as Her Highness."

14

The woman who'd killed my family had hired me to take out the one person who'd known she was guilty. Her Highness had contracted with me to kill her own sister. I felt sick thinking about all the money I'd taken in payment from her. Blood money.

I blinked back tears. "But why did she want us dead? Why didn't she kill me?"

Muriel scooted over to me and patted my hand. It took everything I had not to jerk my hand away from her bony one. "My guess is she would have, had you been there that day. When she had more time to think about it, she realized you could be useful to her later. The earlier jobs she gave you were training for me. She knew you'd want revenge, and that would help kill two birds with one stone so to speak." She smiled weakly. "And you're the second bird. After killing me, she would have called you back and killed you too."

I couldn't believe I'd been so gullible all this time. No wonder she'd promised to deliver the greatest fairytale of all time. "But that doesn't answer the why part about killing my family."

"Evan ... Prince Evan stood to inherit the throne when he came of age. Her Highness has no intention of ever giving up her spot as

Queen. Not that she was even supposed to be Queen anyway. I'm older than her by a year. My crown and scepter were handed down to me from my mother. When she had her own commissioned to look like mine, I thought it was a case of petty jealousy. Until our parents died, and she claimed control of the throne." Muriel sighed and brushed a wiry gray hair from her face. "I never wanted power anyway and didn't want to fight her so I left to live in nature. Seems over time, most people forgot Gertrude ever had a sister...including Gertrude."

Cal's shrieks of laughter pierced the air as Evan gave him a piggyback ride around the grass.

"But how could Evan inherit the throne? He's not really a prince. Our mom and dad weren't royalty."

Muriel looked down. "No, they weren't. But you may well know that the King has always had a hankering for women other than his wife. Especially young, pretty ones. I heard he and his guards were out hunting on horseback one day and came across your mother picking berries. He took her by force while his guards stood by and watched. Your father found her crawling home, battered and bloody. She told him what happened but made him promise not to do anything for fear they'd be killed or banished from Liralelle. Not long after that, she discovered she was with child."

It was difficult to stomach that Evan was the result of the King sexually assaulting my mom. I turned to watch Evan grin and dodge away from Cal's attempts to tag him. Cal's face was pink and sweaty as he raced after Evan again. That kid never gave up.

"He knows," Muriel said. "But he also knows he got all your mom's goodness. He's nothing like that horrid man."

It still didn't totally fit together. I faced Muriel. "The Queen found out about it, I'm assuming, but I don't get how he was a threat to her though. Even if she didn't want an heir to take over the throne, it's not like she can be Queen forever. She has to die at some point."

Muriel's face grew sad, her wrinkles etched deep in her face. "That, my dear, is debatable. Let's just say that while I use my magic for good, she's been using it for other reasons. I've been in hiding for years, trying to find a way to stop her. When I spoke to Helga the night before she died, she described the warrior Bree that she'd met that day, and I knew it was you. We were to meet that night and discuss a plan, but when I arrived, I saw my sister there with Helga."

Muriel wiped a tear from her eye. "The Queen and I fought and my magic prevented her from killing me outright. She threw me against a tree. When I came to, Helga was dead and I couldn't bring her back."

That explained the citrine I'd found on the ground. The force of hitting the tree must have knocked it loose. All this time, I'd thought of Muriel as a monster, and she's been trying to help everyone. She pushed her scepter into the ground and feebly attempted to stand.

"Here, let me help you." I grabbed her arm and helped her up. The bony grasp of her fingers didn't seem as scary now. Her watery eyes seemed kind rather than evil.

"Thank you, child." She smiled at me. "We have to go now."

Evan picked up Cal and tossed him over his shoulder. "Time to move on, kiddo."

We got Muriel's horses ready for travel. She and Evan had one ready for me. Cal rode with me, tucked safely in front, his hands grasping the reins with mine so he could help "steer." Muriel rode just ahead, while Evan's horse stayed in step with my own. The air was cool but comfortable, and trees rustled as a gentle breeze blew through them.

Evan explained that they'd been moving from cabin to cabin in the forest, a series of safe havens that Muriel had set up over the years to prevent discovery. He told me that right after Her Highness had sent me back to my world, she'd asked him who he was. Since he didn't know his true heritage at that time, he'd told her about his adoptive parents, but something told him to leave out the part that he was a prince. He accompanied her to Muriel's cabin only to find it empty. Her Highness had been furious that Muriel had escaped her again. He overheard her tell Rolph that they would return to the castle to gather guards in order to hunt Muriel down.

Hearing Rolph's name made me wistful. Hopefully, he'd realized by now that his employer was not the caring leader she pretended to be. "I hope Rolph is okay."

Muriel called over her shoulder. "He is. Who do you think warned me about your little brother being in danger?"

My heart soared. He had helped to save Cal from Her Highness. But that also meant that he was playing a dangerous game. If the Queen knew about his betrayal, she'd kill him.

"And Ava?" I asked Muriel, a lump in my throat. "Any news about her?"

"I'm hungry," Cal whined.

Evan reached into his pack and produced an apple. He reached over to Cal's eager hand. "Here you go, bro."

"Yes, child," said Muriel. "But I'm not sure what it means yet. Rolph heard guards talking about a kidnapped girl who escaped from Gertrude."

"She got away!" I cried. "That means she's alive."

Muriel hesitated. "Possibly. But Gertie threw a fit about it and has been on the hunt for this girl. She's got her guards combing the land for me as well as your friend."

Cal crunched into the apple, keeping his other hand on the horse's mane. I had a feeling he'd be asking Mom for a pet horse when we returned home. If we returned home. Mom was probably a wreck, and Jay must have realized I was gone by now. Even though the thought was a selfish one, I missed Jay and wished he was here. And I'd do anything to hear Ava's chattering voice again.

"But that means she's out here somewhere."

Evan looked grim. "I've looked everywhere, believe me. No one has seen her in days. If the Queen found her, she'd likely have killed her outright this time."

He was right. Her Highness wouldn't risk taking her back to the castle, not if she was growing more worried about Muriel.

"That's why we're traveling," Evan continued. "We're searching for Ava, but also trying to rouse support from the locals and tell them what's going on. We need to find a way into the Center Village unnoticed. The highest population of Liralelle residents live within the

Village gates. Once they discover that Her Highness is behind the missing girls, we should find many people willing to fight."

Muriel slowed her trot ahead of us. "The problem will be getting in unnoticed. No doubt Gertrude has considered this. Guards are likely placed all along the perimeter."

"I still feel responsible for Ava," Evan said. "I just don't think it's a good sign that no one we've come across so far has seen her. It's not like she knew anyone in Liralelle aside from us. She wouldn't know who she could trust or where to go."

We rode in silence a few minutes. Splatters of sunshine broke through the forest in places where the trees were less dense. My mind wandered, trying to process all of the information I'd absorbed in the past hour. Thoughts of Ava pierced my brain and I remembered how brave she'd been when she first landed in this crazy place. If by chance she was still alive and in the forest somewhere, she'd be dying for someone to talk to.

I jerked my head up. "I think I know where she is."

15

We briefly stopped to let the horses drink, and let Cal run around and expend some energy. He was being so good with all of this. I wondered how long it would take until he asked to see Mom and go home. What would I tell him then? He leaned against me once we were back on the horses. Soon I heard his gentle, even breathing and knew he'd fallen asleep. I placed a protective arm around his waist so he wouldn't slide off.

We rode until we reached the edge of the forest nearest the troll village. The familiar puff of smoke from the fire ring rose into the air.

Muriel chuckled. "Gertrude always hated the troll village even more than the commoners. She'd have sent guards to check it out but wouldn't have gone in there herself. If she's here, your friend is a smart one."

Evan glanced around the clearing to the village. "I don't see any guards, but they could be hiding."

I nodded. "I'll go in. I know the most likely place she'd be." I sat up straighter and tugged on Cal's arm to wake him.

Muriel struggled to dismount her horse, and Evan rushed to her aid. Her crown and scepter stayed hidden in a bag tied to her horse's saddle. "Well, I don't get around as well as I used to these days, but I will remain here and guard the child." She fished a sugared treat out of another pouch and Cal quickly hopped down to take the candy. Nothing woke that kid up faster than sugar.

Evan nodded. "I'll make a ruckus on the far side of the village. If there are any guards, it will draw them over there." He looked toward me. "You slip in through the side. If there are no guards, I'll come back here and wait with Cal and Muriel."

I frowned. "And if there are?"

Evan shrugged. "I'll figure something out. I'm resourceful like that."

"Be careful, Evan. I'm pretty sure Ava wants you alive."

He grinned. "That's what I'm hoping. I owe her for not staying awake. Wait for my signal—you'll know it when you hear it."

Evan took off through the woods toward the back edge of the village. A few minutes later, I heard him whooping and hollering, and singing a song that involved the word 'whiskey.' If I didn't know better, I'd have thought he was drunk. Which I guess was the point.

Nothing happened. No guards stormed out from the woods to apprehend him. No flash of swords could be seen through the thick trees.

I kissed Cal on the top of his head. "Be good."

He nodded while chewing off another piece of candy. Muriel smiled at me. "Nothing will happen to this boy under my watch."

I knew it was true. I thought about the scepter and her crown in the bag. "Can't you and your sister summon each other the way you do with me?"

Muriel shook her head. "Magic is a funny thing. It has rules like everything else. Since we possess the same abilities, they don't work on each other."

"That explains why you've been able to hide from her for so long." I looked at Cal. "Okay, be right back."

I sprinted toward the village, which was only surrounded on the front three sides by a wooden fence. They must have figured that if they were so disliked, they didn't have to worry about keeping people out. No one wanted in to begin with. The back side simply opened up into the forest. I scaled the fence and dropped down on the other side.

A series of small huts lay before me, and I knew the hut I wanted was closer to the front entrance. I skirted between other huts and was passing behind the fire ring when I saw a troll I recognized. Travis. The troll who'd been infatuated with Ava and her hair. Sweat dripped down his face, as he tirelessly chopped wood for the fire. I crept behind a large tree and whisper-shouted to him. "Travis!"

Travis whipped around, raising his axe in the air mid-chop. He looked fiercer and less amiable than last time I saw him. "Travis, back here," I whispered again. "It's me, Bree. Remember, I'm friends with Ava, the blond-haired girl."

Travis lowered the axe and walked toward my voice. He whistled as he walked, as if he were just going to collect more logs for the fire. His face appeared next to mine behind the tree. "It's not safe here, miss," he said quickly. "The Queen's guard 'ave been doing raids at all hours, lookin' your friend. I knew that girl was a good one, that somethin' wasn't right."

My heart hammered in my chest. "Have you seen her? Ava, I mean."

Travis looked around quickly. A few other trolls chopped wood on the opposite side of the fire ring. They sang songs involving activities with the troll women that my mother would have found totally inappropriate. None of them paid any attention to Travis.

"Aye. She's stayin' with Horace. He's been hidin' her and I've been bringing them what they need."

Hope surged through me. I wanted to reach out and hug Travis. "I have to see her."

Travis nodded. "Come back tonight, when it's dark. The raids have all been in the daytime. With having no light out here, 'cept lanterns and sunlight, they can't search very well after sunset."

I'd come so far to find her that waiting several hours felt like torture, but at least I'd see her soon. "Thanks, Travis. If you see her, tell her I'm coming." I leaned over and gave him a quick peck on the cheek.

His cheeks flushed a deep shade of crimson. "No worries, miss. I'm happy to help."

I wound my way back toward the maze of huts. Movement caught my eye in my peripheral vision. Hildegard, the nasty female troll I'd first asked about Horace stood in the window of her hut, a scowl plastered across her face. She pulled the blind down, like she couldn't get me out of her vision quickly enough.

I got back to the fence and hurdled over it. Cal, Evan, and Muriel sat in a circle in the woods, quietly playing a game with sticks. They must have convinced Cal that being loud was dangerous, because I've never heard him silent for longer than a few minutes.

Muriel smiled when she looked up. "I can tell by your face that your friend is okay."

I couldn't contain my grin. "Yeah, but I haven't seen her. We have to camp out for a bit and go in when it's dark. The guards have been doing raids during the day."

Evan pumped his hand in the air. "That's perfect. I can't wait to see her and apologize in person."

Cal's face fell. "Bree, do you mean we have to be quiet all day?"

I squatted down next to him and ruffled his hair. "Yes, but it will be fun ... like a game."

His eyes brightened a little, but he remained doubtful. "I don't think being quiet is very fun."

Muriel opened one of the satchels at her side. "And I have plenty of treats."

I sighed as his face lit up. "Enjoy it while you can, Cal. As soon as we get home, it's back to bananas and oatmeal."

It finally grew dark enough to see the first stars twinkling in the night sky. We ate bread and cheese for supper since we couldn't risk a fire in the dark. The last thing we wanted was attention. We'd had one incident before dusk where several of the Queen's horsemen passed by within fifty feet of where we sat. Luckily, we'd camped in a dense area full of foliage and trees. I'd pulled Cal down into the brush with me and hoped that the horses would stay quiet enough to go unnoticed. The horsemen hesitated a moment and the silence had gone on for what seemed like eternity. They finally continued on through the woods.

Evan lay on the ground next to Cal and pointed out stars visible between the canopy of the tree tops. Dim light from the moon lit the area outside the tree line, and the air was brisk and cool. It was enervating and brought back memories of some of my former missions under the orders by Her Highness. I shuddered to think of those I'd killed at her behest. Those she'd told me were evil and needed to die before they killed others. What if those were lies too and I'd killed innocent people?

Muriel's hand came to rest on my shoulder. "Doesn't do any good to rehash the past, child. Just use what you learned to do better next time."

"What are you, psychic or something?" I asked.

Muriel smiled. "You'd be amazed by how much people's faces give them away. Now you'd best be moving along."

"I'm going with you," said Evan.

I shook my head. "No, it's fine. I'm just going to get her and bring her here. Then Muriel can send her back home with her scepter."

Muriel shook her head. "She won't be any safer in your world than Cal was. Gertrude will find her there, just like she found him."

"Why did she want Cal?

Muriel's voice was slow. "I would have told you already if I knew but I'm not sure. You'd have to ask her that. You'll get the chance, dear, because until we stop her, I don't think he will be safe. In either world."

I felt sick to my stomach. How could I defeat a witch like her? Especially if Muriel's magic didn't affect Her Highness. "What am I supposed to do? I don't want to put anyone else in danger but I don't know how to beat her by myself."

"What do I look like, chopped liver?" asked Evan. "You don't have to do it by yourself."

Muriel's eyes shone in the dark. "I sense you've had many responsibilities in your young life, warrior child. But we all need help at times. Even me." She rummaged through one of her bags as she spoke. "Letting others help when you need it is the sign of a great leader. Gertrude's pride is her weakness."

Evan stood up. "I'm fine with standing guard while you get Ava. Just get back here as fast as you can. We'll figure out a plan after that."

I thought of whom else might be able to help. "Ella would help us, if we can find a way to get to her without her step-sisters seeing. She goes alone to fetch water from the pond."

"That's what I'm talking about," Muriel said. "Every person counts."

Cal held on tightly to my leg. He wasn't as fearless in the dark as he was during the day, and I wished I had a nightlight to turn on for him like I did at home. I hated to let him go. "Stay close to Muriel. I'll be right back."

"You keep saying that," Cal said. "I just want to go home to my bed."

"I know, sweetie. I'm trying to get you there. Hold on a little longer."

Something flashed in the darkness. "Here," Muriel said. "It's a sword. You might need it."

I gripped the cool silver handle. A sense of confidence and calm overcame me. I was still Bree, warrior of Liralelle, and I could save the Kingdom from Her Highness. With help, I reminded myself. I ducked out of the trees and ran toward the troll village.

The fire still burned at the center of the village, casting strange moving shadows over the ground from the flickering flames. The village was eerie at night—silent, save for the crackling of the fire. One lone troll stood at the edge of the fire ring, tossing in logs to ensure it never died out. I stayed close to the huts and made my way toward the front. The huts all looked the same in the dark. I worried I wouldn't know which one was Horace's without light. After weaving around several huts, I recognized Horace and Helga's roses climbing the wall.

My heart raced as I crept to the back of the hut to a small window. Since the trolls were much shorter than me, I had to stoop down to peek inside. The interior still looked warm and cozy. Fresh flowers adorned the table, and the teakettle whistled on the stove. I watched Horace get up from a chair to retrieve the kettle. He poured the water into a teacup. Just one teacup though. Where was Ava? She loved that tea.

I tapped lightly on the open wooden frame. Horace jerked his head toward me, but he wouldn't know it was me in the dark. He confirmed that thought by reaching into a drawer and removing a large knife. My own weapon was sheathed at my side, and there was no way I was using it against Horace no matter what happened. He came toward the open hole in the wall.

"Horace, it's me. Bree."

He stopped halfway to the window, and lowered, but didn't drop the knife. He peered into the night. "If you're Bree, where did you meet Helga?"

"In her shop. The same day she was killed. Muriel came to your house that night."

Horace quickened his pace to the window and leaned out. "It's you! Get in here ... it isn't safe."

He took my hand while I attempted to crawl inside. It was such a small space that I got stuck and wasn't sure I could fit through. I couldn't believe I made it so far only to get stuck in a window frame.

"Here, let me help." Horace yanked me with a forceful pull.

I yelped as I flew through the window and landed on his floor with a thud. My sword clanked loudly on the ground.

"Sorry 'bout that. Just trying to help."

I stood up and brushed myself off. "I know. Please tell me Ava's here?"

Horace's eyes darted around the room like he expected the Queen to appear out of nowhere. "Yes, but a few guards came through today. Searched the house and grilled me up and down. Said someone reported seeing you in the area and wondered if you'd been to see me."

I groaned. "Hildegard. She saw me earlier when I came to find Ava. Did they find her?"

Horace smiled. "Course not."

He motioned me over to a small rug on the floor and lifted it. He took the knife and pried up the edge of one of the wooden floorboards. A small section of the floor popped off, revealing Ava. She sat on a tiny stool, cup of tea in hand. "It's about time, B. I didn't think you'd ever show up."

"A!" I squealed and helped her step out of the tiny hole in the ground before gripping her in a bear hug. "I can't believe you're okay." I squeezed her harder.

"I won't be if you keep hugging me like that," she gasped.

"You don't have much time," Horace warned. "I wouldn't be surprised if the guard returns again. They seemed mighty suspicious of me, and very interested to hear that you were back in Liralelle."

"What's the plan?" Ava asked.

"Basically, to get you out of here, and figure the rest out later. It's all I got." I readied my sword and prepared to leave when I remembered Muriel's words about asking for help. "Horace, you've done so much already and risked your life to keep Ava safe. I hate to ask this, but do you suppose any of the trolls here would be up for a little revolution?"

I briefly described everything I knew about the Queen, Muriel, and the village girls who'd disappeared.

"Wow, Muriel tried to help my Helga that night." Horace became emotional. "You'd think the trolls, of all creatures, would know not to judge a book by its cover." He stroked his chin, deep in thought. "Let me see what I can do. Most trolls in these parts are mighty loyal to each other, Hildegard aside. When they hear what Her Highness did to my wife, they will be fired up to help."

"I know Travis will be, for sure," I added. "If you tell him what Her Highness tried to do to Ava."

Ava's cheeks grew pink. "Oh, yeah, Travis. He's sweet for a troll." She stared at Horace and covered her hand with her mouth. "Sorry, that came out totally wrong."

"No offense taken," Horace said. "But you really have to be going now. I'll send word when I have news. Stick to the forest and we'll find you."

Ava grabbed Horace's hand. "Thank you. For the company, the tea, everything. I owe you so much."

"Just stay alive, little lady. Be safe."

He waved us toward the back window.

"Oh no," I said. "I'm not sure I'll make it through there a second time. We'll take our chances with the door."

Horace opened the front door, and we slipped out into the night. We moved as silently and quickly as possible, staying far from Hildegard's hut. The same troll tossed logs into the fire. I was grateful for the light it provided. The distance to the fence wasn't far and we made sure to stay in the shadows.

I leapt the fence in one smooth movement, while Ava climbed over carefully. "Another reason why you got the lead in the performance," she whispered.

I hadn't given a second thought to ballet. For all I knew, the dress rehearsal had already happened and the lead had been given to Catelyn. I just hoped that Jay hadn't quit the show. There was no reason for both of us to give up our Juilliard dreams.

We made it to the woods. It was hard to discern their figures in the dark until Cal's small voice called out. "Bree, is that you?"

A small lamp lit the circle. Muriel held it to her face. "We're under so much cover here that we should be okay with a little light for a bit."

Ava's face lit up when she saw Evan. "Hi, you."

Evan grinned and picked up Ava in the air. "I'm so glad you're okay. I've been looking everywhere for you."

We all sat in a circle, huddled together. Ava and Evan sat next to each other, both smiling. Cal curled up in my lap and I stroked his hair until I heard his breathing settle into the steady rhythm of sleep.

"What happened that night anyway?" I asked.

Ava's face hardened. "I was sleeping. Next thing I knew, a hand covered my mouth and someone lifted me into the air. I found out later it was one of the Queen's guards. I tried to kick him but he was too strong and I lost my shoe. He gagged me with some nasty cloth and tied my hands together and rode with me on the horse. It wasn't until the guard stopped to let the horse drink from a stream while he went off to um, relieve himself, in the woods, that I had a chance to run.

Ava's words tumbled out in a rush. "I heard his footsteps behind me, but I didn't stop. All I pictured was that girl we found in the woods and I didn't want it to me be. He gained on me since my hands were tied, so I found a large bush and hid underneath it until he passed by. After what felt like hours, I crawled out. I remembered this village but couldn't remember exactly where it was, so I wandered until I saw the plumes of smoke from the fire." She finally stopped for a breath. "Anyway, I'm so happy to see you all."

I couldn't believe everyone was okay. For now. Muriel's face was difficult to read in the light. I told her about Horace and the support we'd likely get from the trolls. "What do you think, Muriel?" I asked. "Where do we go from here?"

"I think we go to your friend Ella and then on to the Center Village. Hopefully, we'll hear from the trolls by then. After that, we take what forces we have, and go after Gertrude." Her mouth was set in a grim line. "We'll see how she likes to be the one being hunted."

Evan grabbed Ava's hand. "The Center Village will be tough but after that, hopefully we should have enough people to take on the Guard. The trick will be staying out of sight."

Cal shifted onto his side, his face angelic as he slept. He wasn't safe with us yet wouldn't be safe back home with Mom either. It was a lose-lose situation and I didn't know how to protect him.

The wind picked up, sending leaves skittering across the ground. As it grew stronger, my hair swirled around my face. Evan jumped up and helped Muriel to her feet. Ava squealed and reached toward Evan. "Is this another one of those tornado things? Is it coming for me?"

"No," Muriel said. "Her scepter can only summon those under contract with her." She stared at Ava. "Well, and anyone near them when the funnel hits. Luckily, my scepter has the same abilities and I can summon anyone she contracts with as well. Gertrude has been forced to go out and find her victims on her own ... or send her Guard."

I couldn't even imagine how many more victims she'd have by now if she could have summoned them at will with her tornado.

The roaring of the wind woke Cal and he shivered. I stood up, not letting go of him. The air around us started rotating. "Then it must mean it's for me," I said. "But how? She released me from my contract when she sent me back home."

Muriel shook her head. "Knowing my sister, she didn't do the actual formal release. She would want to keep you tethered—just in case. She's never been big on keeping her word."

I stared past the lamp light and just made out the angry dark funnel forming behind Muriel. If the funnel hit me, then everyone would end up in Her Highness' grasp. Muriel raised her scepter and drew a circle in the air. A gold light streamed from it and encircled our group in a cylinder of bright, shimmery light. The winds fell calm in the circle, yet the black funnel raged larger beyond it.

Cal stared around wide-eyed. "This is so cool!"

Cool was not the word that came to mind as the funnel slammed against the golden circle. Horrific was more along the lines of what I thought, but Cal probably thought this had to have a happy ending just like in his book. He didn't realize that Her Highness had a very different ending in mind.

We stood there entranced in the magical eye of a storm.

Evan turned in a slow circle. "How long will this thing hold?"

"That's the tricky part," Muriel said. "It can last just as long as her tornado. The problem is that her funnel can last indefinitely."

Ava groaned. "And we can't stay in here forever."

Muriel raised an eyebrow. "Exactly."

16

The safety of the circle seemed like a prison once I realized Her Highness had us trapped. We'd need food and water, not to mention sleep, at some point. She had us where she wanted us versus the other way around. Muriel looked weary even after seating herself in the middle of the circle with the scepter pointed skyward. Tears pricked my eyes when I realized what I had to do. Muriel might be right that I couldn't beat the Queen on my own, but we wouldn't have a shot of survival if we were all imprisoned and killed.

I kissed Cal's head and gripped him fiercely, then let go and placed his hand in Evan's. "You're his big brother now, Evan. Watch over him. Find Ella, get the villagers, and rescue me if you can."

Ava frowned. "What are you talking about? You're right here."

"I'm sorry, A, about everything."

Muriel simply nodded as though in resignation. She knew there was no other way. Her scepter pointed toward the far edge of the circle nearest the funnel. The golden glow dimmed in one section and formed a hole that looked black from the funnel against it.

"I love you all." I ran and dove into the black winds.

. . .

"Well, well, well, someone found their way back to Liralelle without my assistance. I'm ever so curious how that happened." Her Highness sat on her throne, arms crossed, scepter in hand. She'd dropped all pretense of the gracious Queen act.

I stood in the center of the throne room. It was empty save for us, which made me wonder about Rolph. I hoped he was okay. For the first time, I also noted the lack of windows in the room. It hadn't seemed sinister until now.

"Well?" She rapped the scepter against the arm of the throne.

My stomach tied into knots. I felt like a mouse trapped in a lion's lair with no plan of escaping. "Muriel brought me. She said something about the scepters having shared magic and only being able to summon those under contract with you." I lifted my chin. "If you send me away again, she'll just bring me right back."

She slammed the scepter against the throne. "That stupid witch and her spells. She shouldn't have messed in my affairs."

I took a breath. "She was only trying to save people ... from you. Why were you trying to get Cal?"

Her eyes widened. "How did you know—"

My gut clenched. I hoped I didn't just give Rolph away. It wasn't likely that the Guard members would have passed along that information. "Muriel told me. She's a witch like you, so she must have ways of knowing things. But first my brother here in Liralelle, and then you tried to take Cal." My voice broke and I choked down tears. "Why?"

Her Highness rolled her eyes. "Well that explains why I was unable to find Cal in your world. Muriel must be 'protecting' him from me." She leaned down and stared into my eyes. "I was doing you a favor, actually. You see, the original plan was for you to lead me to Muriel, and then I'd kill you after she was dead. But you ended up being exceedingly good at your job, and you're one of the few women who hasn't dallied with my husband."

She sighed. "When I thought we'd found Muriel in the woods that day, I was going to reward you with letting you have your life back ... go to that dance school you blathered on about." She paused.

"But, as you know, we didn't find her, and your little friend ran away, so my good nature evaporated. I figured if I took your brother, it would look like a kidnapping in your world, and you'd be too devastated to think about Liralelle or your friend."

I stared at her, incredulous. "You think I'd just forget about my best friend? And you think I'm stupid enough not to realize that someone here was behind Cal's disappearance? I just had the wrong person all this time." My anger started to outweigh the fear. "I know all about how your husband raped my mother and how you didn't want an heir to take your throne. But why did you kill Snow and kidnap Ava? I bet you're behind the missing village girls too."

Her Highness stood. "I've given you enough answers. You should have left things alone when you had the chance." She called out in a high, loud voice. "Guard!"

Four guards rushed into the room. They were the same ones who always escorted me into the throne room. Though they'd never been nice to me, now they almost snarled at me. Her Highness smiled frostily. "I'm afraid you're all out of chances and I'm fresh out of patience."

A guard took each of my arms. I pulled against them to no avail.

"Take her to the dungeon," she ordered.

I tried to kick the guard to my right, but he moved easily out of my way. They dragged me toward a small metal door behind the throne.

Things weren't going in my favor so far. I yelled over my shoulder at Her Highness. "You won't win this. You thought you could take Ava, but you couldn't. You thought you could kill my brothers ... but you couldn't. I can't believe I ever trusted you."

"Stop!"

The guards halted mid-step and turned me to face the Queen. Her face was like ice. "What did you just say?"

Oh no. Maybe she really had no idea that Evan was still alive. "Um, which part?"

She strode up and bent down toward me, her faces inches from mine. The wrinkles in her face weren't as deep as they seemed last time I saw her. Strange.

Her words were slow and precise. "The part where you said I didn't kill your brothers, as in plural."

I stammered. "I-I'm just saying that my brother Cal is alive, that's all."

Her brows knit together, then her lips stretched into a sinister smile. "I don't believe you. You will give me the information I need, Bree. One way or the other, you will. I promise."

The guards must have taken that as their exit cue. They grabbed me and pushed me again toward the door. We entered into a dim, narrow hallway. They pushed me down a long winding set of stone stairs, and the air grew damper and staler the further down we went. One guard used a large key to open a heavy door at the bottom of the stairs and we entered what had to be the castle dungeon. Her Highness must have gotten some decor ideas from some of her fairytale books, such as the torches lighting the hall and ornate axes hanging criss cross on the wall. However, the long rows of small cells containing only a cot and a bucket seemed more like something out of Alcatraz.

Most of the cells were empty, thank goodness, but I'd been hoping I'd catch a glimpse of someone—maybe one of the missing village girls. The mildew scent assaulted my nostrils and the whole place smelled like decay. The hallway of cells was long and appeared to dead end into large stones a little further down from us. That meant the only way out was through the locked door we'd just come through.

We stopped about three-quarters of the way down the hall. A guard unlocked the cell door. "Here you go. Home sweet home."

The other guard pushed me inside and locked the cell behind me. They chuckled to themselves as they retreated. I heard the faint click of the lock when they passed through the door. They must love the fact that they got to throw me in here. The Queen didn't trust them enough for the big jobs, which was why she'd hired me, but now they got to put me in my place.

I pushed my face to the bars and looked left and right but could only see a few cells down in each direction. A way out certainly didn't present itself. Counting the locked door in the Queen's throne room, the door at the bottom of the stairs, and my cell, there were three doors that I had no key for. I had to hope that Muriel and the others found an unexpected army to help them storm the castle.

I studied my cell. Stone walls made up the other three sides of the room, not a window in sight. The roof was low, maybe eight feet high at most, and was also made of stone. The cot looked dingy but clean. I sank onto it and sighed.

"Bree?"

I looked around.

"Hello?" I called into the air.

"Is that you, Bree?" the voice called again. Their voice had a grating quality to it and I didn't recognize it.

I ran to the narrow bars of my door. "Yes, it's Bree. Who's there?"

"Over here."

I craned my neck and peered to the right, toward the dead-end half of the hallway. A face appeared two cells down diagonal to me.

I'd know that face anywhere. "Rolph!" He looked pale, really pale. "Are you okay?"

"Okay probably isn't the best word to describe me at the moment ... I'm really thirsty."

That explained the rasp in his voice.

"How long have you been here?" I asked.

"Not long. Only a day or two. Once I realized what that woman was up to, I did all I could to help you. She's not dumb and quickly figured out where my loyalties were. Have I mentioned I'd kill a puppy right now for a glass of water?"

I didn't understand how he could be so weak after only a day. "Is she starving you?"

Rolph sighed. "I wish. She'd drinking from me. I'm not sure how much time, or blood, I've got left."

I blinked. "What? Like she's a vampire?"

"No," Rolph said. "Just an evil witch with a relatively new spell. She cuts me and drinks the blood out of one of her crystal glasses. Keeps her young. That witch plans to stay Queen for eternity."

My own blood turned icy. "Oh God, Rolph. That's why she wanted Ava. The missing village girls ... have you seen any girls down here?"

His scratchy voice sounded like it was about to give out. "No. I didn't know this place even existed until recently. Her Bitchness said it was a storage area."

It was—a storage area for girls.

Rolph went on. "After getting a little friendly with a rather handsome guard, I found out that the Guards were taking girls from the village and keeping them here. But the villagers, believing Muriel was behind it, started keeping their kids inside so victims were harder to come by. After draining the imprisoned girls—the Queen got desperate. Apparently, the blood of the young only lasts for so long—so she went out herself to find fresh meat."

My stomach dropped. Those girls were dead. "Snow," I said. "She killed Snow."

I watched Rolph as he sagged against the bars, wrapping his thin, pale fingers around them. My heart broke for him. "Rolph, I know this is obvious, but you're not a girl. Why you?"

A gutteral sound came from his throat. I realized he was trying to laugh. "She said I was the closest thing to a girl she could find. She'll never stop now. No girl is safe."

"What about the King?"

Rolph scoffed. "No one has heard from him in a few days. Some guards think he left Liralelle. My guess is she got fed up with his philandering and took him out. Bree, you have to stop her."

Great. It was hard to stop someone from inside a metal prison. "Doesn't she realize her plan has a serious flaw? She'll run out of girls eventually, right?"

Rolph had sunk to the floor and was resting his face against the bars. "In this world she will ... but then she has yours."

My heart skipped a beat. I remembered the night she traveled to my world to leave me at the orphanage. She'd likely been visiting my world for years, scoping out places where it would be easy for a troubled young teenage girl to disappear. She really could stay young forever, and who knew what damage she could do if her powers kept growing. She'd make our world dictators look like harmless, fluffy kittens.

"I have to get you out of here, Rolph. I'll figure something out." I tried to portray a confidence I didn't feel.

He simply nodded his head before curling up on the floor. "Think I'll just rest awhile now," he mumbled.

I went back to the cot and sat down, my head in my hands. Whatever I did, I'd have to do fast. He wouldn't last another feeding and then she'd be sure to turn to me as her next donor. I knocked on the stone walls. They were thick and sturdy. I'd seen movies where people used eating utensils or homemade shanks to dig holes in the wall over a period of years, but I didn't have years—I probably didn't even have days.

As if on cue, the sound of the door opening echoed down the hall. A guard—one of the same ones that had brought me here—stopped in front of my cell with a large tray. He smirked at me and held up one of the keys from the ring that must have been the one to the cell. "Don't you wish you had this?" he taunted. Though I had no plan, if he opened that door, I would take my chances and run for it. Instead, he slid the tray through a long, narrow opening near the bottom of the door. He chuckled. "Eat up. Tomorrow's a big day for you."

He took the other tray and brought it down to Rolph. "And tomorrow's one of the last days for you." All the guards were pretty bad but this one was awful.

Tears filled my eyes. Her Highness would be back for the rest of Rolph's blood tomorrow, and would probably start on mine. The effects of the blood must only last a few days. The strong aroma of the food hit my nose, and my mouth watered in spite of myself.

Under the tray's lid lay a juicy steak, green leafy salad and fresh assorted fruit. A meal fit for a Queen. Which ultimately, it was. The menu was high in iron, vitamins and minerals that would ensure strong, rich blood when she feasted on it. Silverware hadn't been provided—she wasn't stupid. It wouldn't do any good to refuse it because I was starving and I'd need the strength to get out of here.

I grabbed the steak with my fingers and chewed off a good-sized bite. It was tender and delicious. If this was my last meal, I couldn't have asked for better, though I would have preferred to top everything off with some chocolate mousse. I gulped water from a large cup—she wanted me hydrated—and alternated between mouthfuls of the greens and the steak. I'd save the fruit for dessert.

I tried to think of ways out of here while trying not to think about Mom or Jay and those brown eyes of his. Hopefully, Cal and A were still safe with Muriel. It crossed my mind that I might never dance another day in my life. Ava was right; I couldn't plié my way out of this. Juilliard didn't seem nearly as important as saving my world from a blood-hungry witch.

I popped a grape in my mouth and stood. Though I might never dance at Lincoln Center, ballet cleared my mind and focused me like nothing else. I hummed the tune to Sleeping Beauty and started dancing in the tiny cell.

"Love the music." Rolph's tired voice filtered into my cell. "If I close my eyes, I can almost pretend I'm sitting in my little boutique in the village, fussing over the newest shipment of scarves ..." His voice trailed off.

I spun in a pirouette. "You'll get your boutique, Rolph. I promise." My eyes closed, as I continued humming along to the song in my head. I thought of the real Sleeping Beauty here in Liralelle, and pangs of empathy gripped me. It would be hard to be filled with music but have no outlet. No wonder she roamed the forest, singing to whatever creature she came across. People thought she was crazy, but her only real crime was tone deafness.

An idea formed. It wasn't a great one, but it was something. I grabbed another handful of fruit and relished the sweetness of the strawberries. It would be a shame to waste the rest of it. I used my knuckles to mash the rest of it into a pulpy juice.

It seemed like hours before I heard the click of the door down the hall. I slathered the red juice up and down my arms and smeared some around my mouth. His loud, heavy footsteps grew closer. I let my body go limp in the middle of the cell and lay there on my side, limbs askew. As he reached the door, I held my breath so it looked like I wasn't breathing.

"What the—?"

The keys clanked against the door as he fumbled for the lock. I hoped he'd hurry because I really needed to breath.

He mumbled as he opened and scrambled toward me. "You better not be dead, or Her Highness will have my head." Guess fresh, oxygenated blood was important. I recognized the voice. It was the guard who'd taunted me earlier. He nudged my arm with his foot.

My lungs burned and I'd have to breath in another second. He was bigger than me, so my only chance was to get him off balance.

His finger swiped at the berries on my mouth as he leaned over me. "These aren't even poisonous. I don't–"

My eyes flung open and I inhaled a deep mouthful of air. His eyes widened in surprise as I leaned up on my arms and swung my top leg forward and then kicked back in a sweeping motion as hard as I could against his ankles. He crashed down next to me and his keys skittered across the floor toward the open door. I leapt to my feet to go after them, but he reached out and grabbed my arm. Thanks to the fruit pulp, he couldn't get a strong grip and when I yanked my arm away, it slid easily from his hand.

I sprinted to the door, barely slowing down as I leaned down to snatch the keys. The guard stumbled as he got to his feet. I swung the door shut and fingered through the keys until I had the right one. He swore and charged at the door. I jammed the key in the lock and turned it, hearing the comforting click just as he hit the door with the full force of his body.

"You'll never get away with this," he growled.

I shrugged. "I probably wouldn't have if you hadn't shown me the right key. Thanks for that."

I ran to Rolph's cell but he stopped me before I could get the key ready. "No," he said. He sat cross-legged on the floor in front of the door. "I'm too weak to move and then we'll both get caught. Go and get as far away from here as you can."

The guard screamed for help over and over again.

"Don't worry," said Rolph. "No one will hear him. It's basically sound-proof down here."

I reached for his hand through the bar and squeezed it. "I'm leaving but I'll be back, hopefully before Her Highness realizes I'm gone." With that, I took off down the hall, my feet pounding against the hard, stone floor. The guard hadn't bothered to lock the first door so I didn't have to search for that key. I bounded up the steps two at a time and paused by the door that I knew led into the throne room. I pressed my ear to the door. Surely, she wouldn't still be in there. She'd be more apt to be resting in her chamber until it was time for her next "snack."

I looked through the keys and tried two before the third one slid right in. The lock made a sharp click when I turned it and I held my breath as I opened the door. The room looked empty. Not a guard or a Queen in sight. I crept around from behind the throne, half expecting to see her hand resting on its arm. After ensuring it was empty, I raced across the slippery marble toward the large columns at the far side of the room. Beyond it was another hallway and then the entrance rooms. Beyond that, freedom.

The problem with the distance between me and the front entrance is the guards that were posted along the way. I peered out from behind the large column. At least two guards paced back and forth by the front door. I'd never get out going straight through, and I doubted I'd even make it as far as the entrance rooms. To my left and right were halls that I knew led to a myriad of other rooms, but I had no idea where they went—aside from the one leading to Her Highness' chamber and that was the last place I wanted to go.

I took a guess and went left, trying to ignore the stickiness of my hands and arms from the smashed fruit that was drying in a congealed glaze on my body. Various rooms lined the hall, including a parlor, a library, a conservatory, and a ballroom. Of course, the one room I hadn't seen was a washroom.

The ballroom was mostly empty, save for an ornate chandelier in the center of the ceiling, which meant nowhere to hide, so I opted for the conservatory. A large grand piano was the focal point of the room and behind it, a partially open window. I stole over to the window, which faced the front courtyard. Several guards stood outside the castle entrance. That was unusual.

Whenever I'd come from my world, the courtyard itself was typically empty. The guards often met us at the front door but rarely patrolled the grounds. Her Highness had grown complacent and must have thought herself invincible until Muriel's recent resurgence.

There had to be a back entrance and servant's entrance to the castle, but they would likely be guarded as well. I'd have to find a room along the side of the castle. It's not like they could guard every window—at least I hoped.

Just as I turned away from the window, a growing sound reached my ears. A grating, god-awful sound that no human should hear. No way. This was not happening.

I leaned as far as I dared out the window. Beauty wandered through the castle courtyard, looking lost and confused, yet singing at the top of her lungs. Every guard swiveled in her direction, two of them already holding their hands over their ears.

What was she doing? It would take the guards all of three minutes to get over their annoyance and realize they had a fresh victim for Her Highness. Beauty would be her next unsuspecting beverage supplier.

Sure enough, the guards moved away from the entrance toward her. Guards I hadn't known about appeared from around the castle corners and joined in the effort. Beauty had to have noticed them— she couldn't be that unaware—but she continued to stroll toward the woods and sang loudly as if her life depended on it.

Or maybe my life. Was she doing this on purpose? The guards swarmed from behind her. Just once, she turned and glanced over her shoulder, her head tilted up as though searching the castle windows. Then she disappeared into the woods, with a troop of castle guards following her like some bizarre version of the pied piper. She had to be helping me. It was now or never, because I couldn't let the same thing happen to her that happened to Snow and the village girls. I darted out of the room and down the empty hallway. After I turned the corner, I headed into the first room and dashed to the window.

There was no one on the ground below. Beauty had drawn all of the guards to the front of the castle. Luckily, the window opened easily and I started to climb out before realizing that I had no weapon. How could I fight all those guards with my bare hands?

The room looked like a type of formal sitting room, with a severe looking couch and several straight-backed chairs. An antique table contained only a book and candle. The book wouldn't do much damage but I grabbed the candlestick and tossed the candle as I climbed out the window. The candlestick must have been made of pewter or a similar metal because it felt heavy and substantial in my hand.

I dropped down to the grass in a crouch and crept along the castle wall, following the shrill sound of Beauty's singing. Ear splitting though it was, it was a huge relief to hear her. Other voices rose from the direction of the forest and outbreaks of shouting and yelling soon drowned out Beauty's song. What was going on? When I reached the end of the castle wall and peered around the corner, some sort of whistle sounded and what must have been thirty more soldiers poured out of the castle entrance and headed into the woods. I pulled my head back to avoid detection.

When I dared to peek again, one lone guard remained. He faced away from me toward the direction of all the commotion. I tiptoed up to him, grateful for the soft grass underfoot. It wasn't until I'd almost reached him that he sensed something behind him. Just as he turned, I smashed the candlestick into the side of his head. He slumped to the ground soundlessly. An absurd image of a child's game came to mind, and I could picture Cal proclaiming, "It was Bree in the court-yard with a candlestick."

In the distance, Beauty's singing came to an abrupt halt amidst the cacophony of yells and grunts. A second later, I heard her again.

Instead of a song, it was a long, blood-curdling scream.

17

"No!" I yelled and sprinted into the woods. My heart raced as I ran in the direction of her shrieking. More yelling broke out ahead and it seemed to be coming from several directions. I tore through the trees until I caught a flash of golden hair. Guards flanked Beauty on either side, pulling her by the arms while she tried to back away from them. Other guards looked like they were battling something I couldn't see from the back. I crept closer and gripped the candlestick tighter.

A guard went down in front of me, shouting in pain, and revealing their attacker in the process. It was a troll. I'd never been so happy to see a troll in my life. It took me a second to register that the trees were teeming with trolls. They carried blunt wooden weapons and one troll smashed his baseball-bat looking tool into the kneecap of the man holding Beauty's right arm. The guard yelped and I went after the other guy on her left. He released her arm to grab his sword, but I was faster. I did an échappé leap and came down hitting him square in the forehead with the full weight of the candlestick.

The guard dropped like a stone, as other trolls streamed in from all sides to attack the remaining castle troops.

"Bree!"

I spun around to see Ava flanked by Travis, the troll who'd professed his crush for her, and Helga's husband, Horace. They all held clubs in their hand. "You're okay!" I exclaimed.

"Yeah, and that was a perfect échappé by the way," she said.

I turned back toward Beauty. She gave me a strange smile then turned and ran into the woods. "No," I yelled. "It's not safe out there. Don't go."

A guard gripped my sticky fruit-pulp-covered arm as I attempted to run after her. "You're not going anywhere."

Travis, Ava, and Horace were on the guard in seconds, and Travis delivered a crushing blow to the guard's chest, which looked like it killed him instantly.

Ava hugged me, then stepped away and peeled her hands from my fruit-stained arms. "What on earth is all over you?"

Before I could respond, another batch of guards crashed through the trees. One went after Travis while another attempted to wrench the candlestick from my hand. I yanked my arm away but he grabbed my wrist instead.

A troll jumped on him from behind and something nudged my left hand. Another troll shoved a wooden club into my hand. The guard twisted to pluck the troll off his back with his free hand without letting go of my wrist.

He smirked as he turned back around to face me and reached for his sword. "I have you now."

I smiled. "You think?" I swung my left hand and the club connected with his cheekbone, making a strange cracking sound.

The guard howled and grabbed at his face. Another troll dropped down from a low-lying tree branch and landed on his shoulders, then clocked him in the head with his weapon until he crumpled at my feet.

I swiveled around as Ava swung her club and hit a guard right between his legs. He dropped to his knees as he groaned, his hands covering his crotch. "I've always wanted to do that," she said.

"Where's Cal?" I yelled over Travis' head who had just taken down another guard. "Is he okay?"

"Yes, he's fine," she said over the chaos. "He's somewhere safe—" her eyes darted around at the guards "—with you know who."

I ducked as another guard came at me but was quickly overtaken by a horde of trolls. "And Evan?"

Ava's brow furrowed. "Don't know. He should have been here by now. He was trying to round up people in the town center."

Just when it seemed like we were winning and that the number of trolls outweighed the number of guards, the galloping sound of horses thundered through the forest accompanied by the war cries of Her Highness's soldiers. The troops on patrol around Liralelle must have been alerted or somehow summoned. They crashed through the trees, brandishing large swords.

Great. There must have been twenty more guards to contend with, and all I had was a club and a candlestick. The trolls whooped and charged the soldiers, undaunted by their small stature as compared to the mounted soldiers. Several trolls went down in a pool of blood from enemy swords just as a horse charged me. The guard's eyes gleamed as he readied his sword to slice me in half. He didn't seem worried about saving me as a meal for the Queen. Maybe her orders had changed.

I dove for a tree, dropping the candlestick on the way, and managed to bring the club over my head for protection just as he swung down. The sword sliced through the air and became embedded in the trunk a few inches above my head. As the guard directed the horse to circle back around, I jumped up and yanked the handle in a desperate attempt to free the blade from the tree. A sword would make a much better weapon than what I had. I jiggled the blade back and forth in a frantic motion as I scanned the area.

Other guards on horseback had encircled a group of trolls, including Travis, and one soldier had caught Ava by the hair and was pulling her toward him. She batted at his arm with her club but another guard reached over and jerked the weapon from her hand.

The guard who had lost his sword in the tree reached down and pulled a smaller knife from his riding boot. The horse stood waiting for a signal from its owner. The guard dug his heels into the horse's side and it came back at me full speed. Though the sword had loosened a little, it wouldn't give way in time and my club was on the ground. It didn't look like this would end well.

Another horse broke through the trees right in front of the charging guard. Evan's blade sliced the man's neck before he even had the chance to look surprised. I never thought I'd be happy to see a prince coming to my rescue, even if it was my own brother, but I'd take it at the moment. Evan was followed by a slew of others who must have been from the village, as I didn't recognize most of them. Ella was among them, and my heart sank when I spotted Red. Some were on foot, others horseback, and they wielded a variety of makeshift weapons.

"Good to see you, bro," I shouted. The horses surrounding the trolls turned to face the onslaught of new attackers.

Ava's eyes lit up as Evan galloped toward the man gripping her hair. She reached up and pulled hard on the guard's arm, which caused him to tilt forward on the horse. He fought to regain his balance as Evan reached him and finished him with his sword, then turned to face the multitude of other guards around him.

The trolls and villagers clashed with the Queen's guard. With a final tug, I freed the sword from the tree, located the fallen guard's knife, then jumped onto the first guard I came across. Everything was a blur of clashing swords, yelling, and falling bodies. It was hard to keep track of how many of the fallen were us versus them.

A strangled shout came from nearby and I turned. Evan lay on the ground near me, a guard's boot across his throat and a sword about to be driven through his heart. Ava pounded on the guard's back with her club to no avail. I lunged and threw the knife, piercing the guard's jugular. He stumbled and tried to stem the flow of blood with his hand but bled out quickly.

I ran to help Evan to his feet. "There, now we've saved each other. We're even."

"Thanks, sis," he said, rubbing his neck.

A sword sliced the air and caught my arm, causing a thin stream of blood to ooze through my shirt sleeve. I swung my sword wildly and caught the man in the thigh. More guards came toward us and a tangle of bodies lay on the ground. A current of air lifted my hair and grew in strength. I gulped. This could be either really good or really bad.

When the air turned black and began rotating, I had my answer.

18

The guards backed away from the funnel and a momentary lull in the fighting occurred as the tornado touched down. I couldn't be summoned now—I was needed here to help fight. Dirt, leaves and twigs swirled before being sucked into the vortex of dark wind. I reached for the nearest tree as though I could latch myself onto it and not get sucked into the funnel.

The funnel grew pitch black but then lessened in intensity. That had never happened before. When the winds died down, they revealed a limp figure lying in the middle of where the funnel had been.

"Rolph!" I rushed to his side. He was unmoving and extremely pale. I felt for his pulse, and it was so weak, I wasn't sure it was there at all. "He needs help!" I yelled to no one in particular. I'd never even seen a medical center in Liralelle—everything was done though spells and witchcraft. Maybe Muriel could help him if I could get him to her.

I knew Rolph had been contracted to Her Highness as a servant, which explained why she could transport him through the funnels, but why send him here? Ava and Evan bent over Rolph.

"Why would she send him here?" Evan asked, echoing my thoughts, as he smoothed Rolph's hair out of his face.

"To distract you, of course." I looked up and Her Highness stepped from behind a nearby tree, with yet more guards at her side. Her guards seemed to multiply like rabbits.

She wore her crown and her best jeweled robes, her scepter raised high in the air with a strange dark green light emanating from its tip. I'd never seen that light before but knew it couldn't be a good thing.

"Where is my dear sister?" she demanded.

"I don't know" I said, grateful that she didn't know either, as it meant Cal was safe with Muriel ... for now.

Her Highness raised her scepter higher in the air. "That's unfortunate."

Rolph remained motionless on the ground and I knew he didn't have much time, if any, left. The other guards stared at her, as though waiting for a command. The remaining trolls and villagers looked to me for guidance, but I had no idea what to do next. So much for my warrior reputation. Without warning, Horace rushed toward the Queen with his club raised. "This is for my dear, sweet Helga!"

Her Highness pointed the scepter at Horace as she whispered a word I couldn't hear. The green light streamed from her scepter like a laser and hit Horace in his chest. His mouth formed a silent scream as he disintegrated into a pile of ash. My stomach dropped. Poor, good-hearted Horace. All I could cling to was that he and Helga were together again.

Movement caught my attention in my peripheral vision, to the right of the Queen. Red pulled a small blue flask from her skirt. *No!* I wanted to scream out but it was too late. She sipped from the vial that I'd given her to save herself from Muriel and morphed into the snarling two-headed creature.

Her Highness laughed. "Guards, I think you can manage to take care of a mere child."

Two guards near her drew their swords, and I glanced around. It was so quiet. Everyone seemed frozen in place, their eyes fixed on the

Queen. Ella met my gaze and nodded. She pulled the lavender bottle I'd gifted her from the bosom of her dress and took a quick pull. In an instant, she disappeared at the same time that Red lunged toward Her Highness with a loud growl.

One of the guards by Red was suddenly lifted in the air and tossed to the ground by unseen forces, a look of shock upon his face. The sword was removed from his hand and appeared to move through the air on its own, suspended several feet above the ground. Though the other guard looked bewildered, he lunged and struck his sword toward the fierce creature that was Red. The blade sliced through the Red's midsection.

"Red!" I screamed and ran.

Everyone snapped out of the frozen silence and the clashing started again. A flurry of trolls, villagers, invisible Ella, Ava, and Evan tangled in battle with the guards. I leapt over a guard on the ground, and sprinted full speed toward where Red lay bleeding on the ground. It might be too late to save Rolph, but maybe I could help Red. The Queen pointed her glowing scepter toward Ella's invisible form wielding the sword. The dark greenish light missed Ella but hit the tip of the sword. Ella dropped the sword with a shriek as it burned her hand before turning to dust.

Right as I reached Red, who was changing back into her normal childlike form with blood oozing from her stomach, the Queen aimed her scepter at me. A greenish light centered on my chest. I was one command away from being turned to dust.

"Drop your weapon, girl," she said coldly. She waved her scepter at Red. "Or I'll turn your little friend there into a pile of nothing."

I looked at Red, groaning in pain on the ground. I tossed my sword to the side, which was immediately snatched up by a guard.

The Queen's smile was icy. "Thank you. If only you could have been more obedient before this." She leveled the scepter at me and the tip glowed green again.

"Leave her alone, you ole' hag. I'm the one you want." Muriel walked out into the clearing. Where was Cal?

Her Highness whipped her head around to face her sister. "You."

She swung the scepter toward Muriel.

Muriel chuckled. "You wrinkled bat ... you know your magic won't work on me."

"Stop. Calling. Me. Names." The Queen's eyes darkened and she directed her scepter at a tree branch hanging over Muriel's head.

Muriel rolled her eyes as the large branch fell. With a quick move of her own scepter, the branch evaporated into gold dust before it reached her. "Is that the best you got, you dilapidated crone?"

Several of the guards had stopped battling trolls and looked toward the Queen for guidance. "Stop staring at me, you fools," she said. "Get her."

The guards rushed Muriel, the trolls went after the guards, and Evan, Ava, and a now visible Ella raced toward me and Red. The guards bounced off of Muriel, likely due to a spell, and Muriel walked slowly toward the Queen. Her Highness's focus was solely on Muriel, her knuckles white from the intense grip on her scepter. It was my only chance.

I ducked low and rushed the Queen. She whipped her head back toward me as I slammed into her body and we crashed to the ground. The impact caused her crown to fall off. I heard a yelp from Ava and looked sideways. A guard had grabbed her and pushed her up against a tree. Evan and Ella closed in on him, weapons in hand. The Queen struggled underneath me and I pinned her arm holding the scepter to the ground before she could turn me to ash. She used her other hand to jam her crown back onto her head.

As soon as her crown was back in place, the scepter glowed and shot out its lethal blackish green light. Luckily, it was still flat on the ground so it shot in a straight line and hit the boots of a guard going after Muriel. He immediately turned to dust.

Her Highness yelled in frustration and dug the nails from her free hand into my scalp. My grip on her loosened despite my best efforts just as a troll rolled over and sunk his teeth into the Queen's wrist that held the scepter. She shrieked and the scepter fell from her hand and rolled about a few inches away in the dirt. All I had to do was grab it and incinerate the evil witch.

I scrambled off the Queen who was also reaching for the scepter. A guard got to it first. He smirked and pointed it at me. Crap. Nothing happened and he looked puzzled. He shook the scepter and pointed it at me again.

"Give it to me!" Her Highness screamed, getting to her feet while holding the crown steady on her head.

Right. The crown. Anyone under contract with the Queen could use the scepter but they also had to be wearing the crown. Travis the troll ran by, jumped up in the air, snatched the scepter from the guard's hands, and kept right on running. He disappeared into the woods, followed by a multitude of guards.

"Go, Travis!" Ava yelled.

Her Highness stomped her foot. "Catch him!"

Muriel had created a golden force field around her. The guards kept trying to run and pierce it with their swords but were thrown onto the ground by the field over and over again. It would have been amusing if Rolph weren't lying dead or dying, and Red wasn't bleeding everywhere. Suddenly, Muriel evaporated into a golden funnel. I turned toward Her Highness. Though I had no idea where Muriel went, I knew one thing for sure. I needed to kill one last witch and end this once and for all—end the witch who killed my parents in cold blood.

The Queen faced me, fury in her eyes and determination in her jaw. She came at me with her bare hands. Everything seemed to go in slow motion. Several quick flashbacks flitted through my mind. A move that Adrian once taught me. One he'd said I wouldn't be able to perfect until I was more advanced in my technique. A story I'd read online about a ballerina who had fought off an attacker with the move. A sudden surge of energy jolted me as the Queen ran toward me, her hands in front of her as though she planned to choke me to death. I jumped back a few feet until my right hand grazed the nearest tree. It was all I had for support and I moved my feet slightly into position.

My right leg shot out in front of me as she closed in. It was a strong, high kick and caught her square in the neck. Her head bounced back and she fell limply to the ground. The guards who hadn't followed Travis and the scepter stopped fighting the trolls to stare at their Queen.

"Oh my gosh, that was a perfect *grand battement!*" Ava yelled in awe. "Brava, Bree!"

Evan used the opportunity to disarm several nearby guards and tossed a sword to Ella who gulped more potion before dropping another handful of surprised guards. The trolls took care of more of them, as the guards seemed unsure what to do without guidance from their Queen.

"Is she dead?" one of the guards asked.

Please let her be dead. The trolls protected me with their clubs raised toward the few remaining armed guards. I leaned down and felt the Queen's wrist. A faint pulse thrummed beneath the surface. "No, I think I just knocked her out really good," I said. Disappointment flooded me that I hadn't killed her, followed by guilt that I wanted someone dead that badly.

A troll tossed me a sword that I caught easily with one hand.

"Finish the witch!" another troll shouted.

I stood over the woman who had taken my first family from me and who'd tried to kill Ava, Cal, and Rolph as well. Anger rushed through my veins and my vision blurred for a moment. I shook my head and raised the sword into the air, ready to thrust it through her evil, lying heart.

A shimmering cyclone appeared and touched down a few feet away. I wanted to cry in relief when Muriel and Cal stepped out from it.

"Cal!" I smiled. "You're okay."

His eyes widened in horror as he took in the scene before him. Dead and injured bodies lying around with his big sister in the center of it all, looking like she was about to murder a sleeping woman with a sharp sword.

"Bree?" he asked, a questioning look in his eyes. He took a step away from me, backing into Muriel.

My stomach lurched and I lowered the sword. No matter how

justified it was, I couldn't kill someone with my little brother watching.

"Tie her up," I ordered.

Evan yanked vines overhanging from the trees and Ava helped him bind the Queen's hands and feet, while the guards looked at each other in confusion.

I dropped the sword and rushed to Cal, then embraced him in a bear hug. "I'm so glad you're okay and so sorry you had to see all this."

He hesitated a minute before hugging me back. "I'll be alright." He looked up at me and smiled. "Also, traveling in tornadoes is really cool."

I ruffled his hair and gently turned him away from the carnage.

Muriel's eyes glistened as she watched us. Several guards backed away from her, bumping into each other. The Queen must have done a good job convincing them that Muriel was evil. I'd blame it on their lack of intelligence but I'd fallen for the same thing.

She wore her crown and held her scepter, which glowed gold at the tip, instead of dark green. "No need to be afraid of me," she clucked at the guards, "unless you mean to do harm to any of my friends here."

My friends. Several of them had already been harmed. I pulled away from Cal and rushed over to Red where Ella sat, smoothing back Red's hair. "Everything is gonna be okay, little one," Ella said to her in a soft voice.

I looked up at Muriel. "Can you help Red and Rolph?" I begged her.

Rolph lay about twenty feet away but had not cried out or moved at all as far as I could tell. Ava and Evan leaned down, and Ava grabbed his hand. "Rolph?"

There was no response.

Ava's lower lip trembled. "He was so nice."

Muriel bent over Red and pointed her scepter at the little girl's gaping wound. Golden flight flowed from the scepter and into Red. The blood flow coming from her stomach slowed but I couldn't tell if that was due to the scepter's magic or the fact that Red was almost out of blood. Then I gasped. The wound began to heal in front of us. Golden light seemed to emanate from every pore in Red's tiny body. Her groans stopped and she placed her hand lightly on her stomach.

A ghost of a smile formed on her pale face. "It doesn't hurt anymore," she whispered.

"Good, that's my girl," Ella said, squeezing her hand. "Told ya you'd be fine."

Several of the guards gasped at what they'd just witnessed. The trolls looked as though nothing could surprise them. Seemingly satisfied, Muriel nodded and hobbled over to Rolph.

Red's eyes sought mine. "Did you get her, Bree? Did we win?"

I wiped tears from my eye. "Yep, I think we got her Red."

She gave a small fist pump in the air. "I knew it. I knew you'd get her. I was brave, huh?"

"Yeah, you were brave." I smiled wanly. "But that's the last time I'm giving you any potions."

I looked over at Rolph and my heart sank. "I'll be right back, Red. Ella will stay with you." Cal ran and clung to my arm. I wished I could cover his eyes so he wouldn't see all this.

Ava and Evan gave Muriel room. The trolls watched intently as Muriel hunched down over Rolph's body and pressed her fingers to his neck.

Please. Please let him be alive.

Muriel slowly shook her head. "I'm afraid he's gone."

A sob tore from my throat. "No!" Not Rolph—not kind, funny, wanna-be-boutique owner Rolph.

Ava looked down at the ground, for once knowing there was nothing to say. Evan held her hand, head bowed. Cal's small hand squeezed mine.

I let my tears fall freely. So many things had gone right. Ava, Cal, and Evan were safe, Her Highness was caught, and the young women of Liralelle could once again sleep safely at night. Yet nothing felt right with Rolph being dead.

I'd failed.

19

M uriel's scepter glowed as she moved it in a giant oval, encircling Rolph's body in a wash of gold light.

"Don't know how long he's been gone," she said. "This might not work."

The flashback of seeing my parents dead popped into my head. Muriel had told me they were too far gone for her to bring them back. My eyes met Evan's. He'd been dead too—just not as long as our parents. Maybe there was still hope.

The light swirled around Rolph, almost obscuring his body from view in the shimmering mist. Muriel's face was grim above him. "It doesn't look good. If nothing else, this energy will help him move on peacefully to what lies beyond."

I didn't want Rolph anywhere "beyond," I wanted him here. I reached into the gold mist and grabbed his hand. "C'mon, Rolph. Come back to us. Please."

The mist gradually settled and appeared to soak into Rolph's body. His skin glowed a beautiful gold hue and a peaceful expression blanketed his face. At least he looked at rest. I couldn't hold it together anymore and sobbed into my hands. Cal stood in silence next to me. I thought of all the adventures Rolph would never have.

"I'd cry too if my hair looked that atrocious."

Huh? I looked down. Rolph's eyes could barely focus yet they were aimed in the general direction of my hair. His voice was little more than a whisper. I threw my arms around him. "Rolph! You're alive!"

He coughed. "Easy, there. I'm pretty sure I'm just barely alive."

"Sorry." I loosened my grip but didn't let go.

Muriel leaned down and patted his hand. "Don't move yet. The magic needs a little more time to work on you. Just rest a bit."

Rolph closed his eyes. "You don't need to tell me twice." He drifted off but the steady rise and fall of his chest was a huge relief.

Cal stared wide-eyed at Muriel. "You are the awesomest witch ever."

Muriel chuckled. "I do my best, child."

The trolls looked in amazement at Rolph and even the hardened Ella had gasped from her spot at Red's side.

One of the guards cleared his throat and addressed Muriel. "I don't understand what's going on here. You just saved that little girl and the Queen's attendant ... but Her Highness said you were the most evil witch of all times and that you wanted to demolish her kingdom."

Muriel put her hand on her hip and stared defiantly at the guard. "Do you have rocks for brains? It's your so-called Queen who is evil. She's behind all this mess—and she's the one whose been taking and killing those village girls."

I frowned at the guard. He seemed to be telling the truth but I knew at least some guards had to know about Her Highness because they'd been working down in the dungeon where I—and the other girls—had been kept prisoner. I told the guard as much.

"What dungeon?" he asked.

The guards exchanged confused looks, until one spoke up. "I never heard about a dungeon but I bet it's the Throne Guard—they are the only four guards allowed in the throne room and in her personal chambers. They don't talk much to the other guards. They went after that troll who took the Queen's scepter."

That made sense since I knew the door to the dungeon was behind the throne. It also explained why those four guards always seemed so much nastier than the rest. Muriel explained everything to the guards who seemed genuinely shocked. Several of them even bowed down to her.

Muriel waved them up with an impatient sweep of her hand. "Don't wanna be Queen ... don't have the inclination nor the patience." She pointed her bony finger at Evan. "That young man is the rightful heir to the throne."

Evan's eyes widened. "I don't think—"

"Nonsense," Muriel interjected. "It's your right and your duty." She nodded toward a guard. "Bring me Gertrude's crown."

The guard hesitated and looked at the unconscious Queen tied up on the ground.

Muriel sighed. "She ain't gonna bite you. Get her crown."

The guard took the crown and handed it to Muriel. She reached into her skirts and pulled out Gertrude's scepter—the one Travis had taken when he ran into the woods.

"What happened to Travis?" Ava asked. "Is he okay?"

"Wasn't about to let those guards hurt that troll," Muriel said. "That's why I left. I had to take care of some guards and then I brought Travis with me to Fibb's place. Fibb was watching Cal for me 'til things were safe ... don't worry, the strongest thing he gave him to drink was cola. Travis is still there."

"Yep, Fibb gave me cherry soda," added Cal, smiling. "It was awesome."

"C'mere, young man." Muriel stood with Gertrude's crown and scepter in each hand.

Evan walked with slow steps over to Muriel. "I'm really not sure I'm ready for this."

"No one's ever ready for something like this," she said, shrugging. "You get used to it after the fact. Now let's get this over with."

"Wait!" I yelled, remembering the blackish green light of the scepter and the black tornadoes. "Aren't her scepter and crown evil?"

"It ain't things that are evil; it's the person using 'em." Muriel placed Gertrude's crown on Evan's head and asked him to hold out his right hand.

Evan placed his hand palm up in front of Muriel. It was a surreal moment. Ella had propped Red up to a seated position, Ava beamed at Evan like a proud girlfriend, and the trolls and guards surveyed the scene in silent respect. Rolph would be upset that he slept through something as important as a coronation—and that he couldn't have styled Evan properly beforehand.

"Do you solemnly swear to rule over the land of Liralelle and all of its inhabitants with justice and fairness?" Muriel asked.

"I do," said Evan, hand still outstretched.

"And do you swear to protect and serve all those that live in this land at all costs?"

"I do," said Evan, looking Muriel directly in the eye.

"And do you promise to use your powers only for good and that no harm will come to Liralelle on your account?

"Yes, I do."

Muriel placed the scepter into Evan's hand. "Then you are hereby pronounced the new ruler of Liralelle." She turned to address the rest of us. "All hail King Evan."

Everyone bowed down toward Evan, who looked uncomfortable with his sudden promotion. I exhaled in relief when the tip of his scepter glowed a similar gold color to Muriel's.

Evan surveyed the assortment of people and trolls around him before focusing on the guards. "If any of you do not support me as King, please speak now. I will hold no ill will and will release you from service immediately. You will be free to pursue other interests, as long as they do not conflict with the greater good of Liralelle."

One guard stepped forward. "Your Highness, with due respect, I never wanted to be a guard. Her Highness—er, Gertrude—forced me into it. I am but a simple man and only want to return to my family and our farm. The food we grow provides for the kingdom, and we sell it in the market at the Center Village. I'd be happy to send some of our best vegetables to you in gratitude."

Evan nodded. "Of course, and you owe me no debt aside from your loyalty."

Another guard piped in. "Take the vegetables, trust me. They're delicious."

Evan smiled. "Twist my arm. Okay, anyone else?"

The other guards remained silent. One looked around and said, "I think I speak for all that it would be an honor to serve you." He cleared his throat. "If I may offer an opinion, I don't think you should offer the same kindness to the Throne Guard though."

I thought of how they had relished throwing me in the dungeon and were so cruel to Rolph. I didn't want to imagine how bad it had been for the girls who'd suffered by their hand. "I agree," I said. "Does anyone know where they would be right now?"

Muriel smiled. "Don't matter where they are. They are under contract to the ruler of the land, which means King Evan here can summon them here. We have plenty of guards here to help subdue them when they get here."

A troll spoke up. "Don't forget us. We'll help too, but ..."

"Yes?" Evan asked. "Speak your mind."

"Well," the troll said, "my name is Hector, and it's just that we haven't always had the best relations with the castle."

"With anyone really, for that matter," another troll added.

Hector nodded. "Right, and we'd like that to change. We'd like to be seen as equals ... we don't want to be taxed higher than the other creatures here. We want the same rights as them."

"And we want to marry whoever we want," another other troll added.

Evan looked thoughtful. "Those rules never made much sense to me anyway. Your request is granted."

A chorus of whoops and hollers came from the trolls.

"So, King Evan ...," Muriel smiled when the racket died down, "... before you deal with the Throne Guard, what do you propose we do with Gertrude there?"

Evan looked down at the former Queen lying in the dirt. "Well, we shouldn't let her dungeon go to waste, should we?"

20

W e sat in the grand dining hall of the castle. It struck me that in all my years of service to the former Queen, I'd never once been invited for a meal. A parade of meats, cheeses, roasted vegetables and fruits were brought in by the castle waitstaff. Evan sat at the head of the table with Ava to his left and Muriel next to her. I sat on Evan's right with Cal by my side. Several times during the meal, Evan reached over to squeeze Ava's hand. I could almost see her squealing inside her head that her boyfriend was a King.

Rolph still slept soundly in his quarters. Before dinner, I'd covered him after sponging some broth into his mouth. He'd murmured something about my hair before falling back asleep. Muriel said it would take a few days for him to fully recover.

It had been an eventful few hours. Ella had brought Red home and offered to stay with her as long as necessary. I was willing to bet it might be a permanent move as the two had bonded quickly, and Ella had been looking to leave her stepmother anyway.

Beauty was found unharmed and singing to a herd of scared sheep. Evan decided to have the castle musician give Beauty formal music lessons for free to give her a sense of purpose ... and improve her craft. Gertrude and her Throne Guard were safely locked away in the dungeon. Evan knew they couldn't stay there forever, but it wasn't safe for the citizens of Liralelle for them to be released. That was a problem for another day.

My mother had to be going crazy at home and I didn't know how much time had passed there or if she even realized I was gone, but I had to get back there with Cal as soon as possible. I'll admit that I also really wanted to see Jay. Strangely, thoughts of ballet were further from my mind than I'd thought they'd be. For all I knew, I'd even missed performing the lead in Sleeping Beauty. I looked around the table. My brothers and best friend were okay, and the girls of Liralelle didn't have to fear being hunted anymore. That was way more important than a play.

Evan had insisted we dine with him before leaving. From the way Ava looked at him, she didn't want to leave at all. With everything that was going on at home, I didn't blame her. Several waiters brought in plates of desserts with a variety of cakes, sorbets, and chocolates.

"This is the best place in the world!" Cal yelled, causing laughter.

Evan clinked his spoon against the glass. "Attention, all. I'd like to make a few toasts. One, to Muriel for her courageous acts in helping us to defeat Gertrude."

"Here, here" said Ava, as we all took a sip of our sparkling pear juice.

"Just doing what anyone would have in my position," said Muriel. "But thank you."

Evan raised his glass again. "Finally, to Bree, warrior of Liralelle ..."

"Um, can I stop you for one sec?" I asked. "Can I just be Bree now? Please."

Evan smiled. "Sure, sis, whatever you want." He cleared his throat. "Finally, to Bree—killer ballerina extraordinaire—whose dedication and bravery has rooted out many evil witches and creatures throughout Liralelle over the years in order to bring peace and safety to our land. Today, she succeeded in bringing down the worst evil Liralelle has ever known. Cheers to Bree!"

"Yay, Bree," Cal clapped, while Ava whistled.

Muriel laughed. "I hope you don't normally have to use ballet for killing."

I shook my head. "Thankfully, no. And I couldn't have done it without help. From all of you. I'm so lucky to have family and friends like you." Tears sprang to my eyes.

"Bet you didn't realize you had family in such high places," Evan teased. "Don't go thinking you're going to get all these special favors or anything."

Ava laughed and playfully punched Evan's arm. "We better all get special favors."

I stood up. "I hate to say this, but we have to be getting back."

Cal looked around the table. "But we can come back to visit anytime, right?"

"Only if I'm summoned." I frowned. "I guess I'm only used to being summoned when things are going badly."

"Well that's going to change," Evan announced. He over looked at Ava. "And I'm going to have to contract you to be my personal assistant or something, because I'm going to want to summon you often."

Ava blushed a deep red color as he took her hand.

Muriel chuckled. "No need for all that. We don't want to disrupt your lives more than they have been already."

"No, I'm fine being disrupted as much as you want." Ava protested.

Muriel reached into her pockets and pulled out two perfect gemstones. They looked almost like—

"Are those from your crown?" I asked.

"Yes, they are," Muriel replied. "Don't worry, my crown still works just fine." She handed one gemstone to me and the other to Ava. The brilliant pink stone shimmered in my palm. "I used my scepter to put a little spell on them. If you hold the stone and wish to be in Liralelle, you will be. So, you can visit anytime. You'll still need one of us to send you back again though."

"Thank you," Ava and I said in unison. I tucked the crystal into my pocket.

"Cool," said Cal. "I'm coming every day!"

"Sorry, little guy," Muriel said. "I don't want you sneaking off and scaring your mom or Bree. The magic only works for Bree, but she can bring you with her."

Cal crossed his arms and glared at me like it was my doing. "Fine, but you have to bring me here a lot. We have a brother here too, you know?"

I smiled. "I know we do. We'll come whenever we can."

"Can Mom come too?" Cal tugged at my shirt. "She'd like this place."

My eyes met Muriel's. "That is for you to decide, child," she said.

"We'll see," I told Cal.

There was one person I wanted to see before we left. "I'll be back in a minute."

I knocked lightly on Rolph's door. "Rolph, you awake?" I whispered as I pushed the door open a few inches.

"Come in," he croaked.

The stable boy sat by the side of Rolph's bed. Rolph was propped up on pillows while the young man spoon-fed broth into his mouth, then wiped his mouth with a napkin. "Give us a moment please, Henry," Rolph said.

Henry ran his fingers over Rolph's face and nodded at me as he exited the room.

Rolph patted the bed next to him.

"And here I thought you were all sick and miserable," I said as I hugged him gently. "Does this mean you and Henry are giving it another go?"

Rolph's voice was weak but clear. "I guess absence really does make the heart grow fonder. We'll see what happens." He reached for my hand. "And don't think I don't know that you're the reason I'm alive."

"No, I'm not," I said. "Muriel is the reason you're alive. She saved you."

"If you hadn't been the one to stop that old hag, we'd all be dead by now. You don't give yourself enough credit," he said. "I'm afraid you're here to say good-bye ... and I haven't even had time to deal with this." His fingers swept my wild curls out of my face.

I swiped his hand away from my hair. "Sadly for you, I can come back anytime I want now to bother you." I explained the power of Muriel's stone.

Rolph flashed a weary smile. "That's great news, you can come for the opening of my new boutique when I'm ready. I'm going to have a whole line of hair care products."

I laughed and kissed his cheek. "I wouldn't miss it. Take care of yourself, Rolph."

Back in the dining hall, Ava, Evan and Cal were racing around playing tag and Cal's laughter echoed across the marble.

Muriel stood off to the side with Roly and Beatrice, the two who normally presided over the formalities after I'd completed another mission for the former Queen. They looked over my way and Beatrice nodded. She shook hands with Muriel and then Beatrice and Roly exited the room. Weird.

Muriel held a bag in her hand as she approached me. She held it out to me.

"What's this?" I asked.

"An additional payment, child. By taking down Gertrude, you ensured the safety of Liralelle for years to come." She opened my hand and plopped the heavy bag of gold into my palm.

"But I can't take this. Gertrude already paid me for finding you ... it still hurts to think how close I came to killing you."

Muriel's eyes were kind. "No use wasting energy over what could have been. I'd say it all worked out pretty well in the end."

"Plus, I didn't kill Gertrude—she's still alive."

"If you call living in a dungeon alive, so be it, but you took care of her so she can't hurt anyone else. I'd say you've more than done your job. Now take it, child. Ava told me about that ballet school you want to go to."

I stared at the amount of gold in my hand. Not only would it fund Juilliard, but my mom could cut back on her work hours—heck, she wouldn't have to work at all. I couldn't comprehend how much this helped my family.

"Thank you, Muriel. I don't know what else to say."

"Nothin' else to say. Good luck, child."

I hugged the old woman. "Please watch over Evan."

"Oh, I will," she said. "He already asked me to move in here and help around the castle. He's going to ask the couple who raised him to live here too. Now are you ready?"

I sighed. "Yes."

We walked back over to Cal, Ava, and Evan. "It's time, Cal," I said.

Evan picked up Cal in a giant bear hug. "I'll see you soon, little guy."

"Promise?" Cal asked.

"I promise," Evan said.

Evan picked up Ava's hand and kissed it. "And you, m'lady, I hope to be seeing you soon as well."

Ava giggled. "Oh you will."

I hugged Evan. "You're going to be a great King."

"Yeah, I'll try not to let it get to my head," he said, hugging me back. "Take care, sis. Don't be a stranger."

Cal gripped my hand in his and sighed. "Okay, I'm ready."

Ava looped her arm in mine and gazed wistfully at Evan. "I guess I'm ready too."

"I'll show you how it's done," Muriel said to Evan.

She said the words I'd heard countless times before from Gertrude's lips. "Return to your world far from here but hold your love for Liralelle near."

Ava blew Evan a kiss as the golden tornado swallowed us whole.

21

We landed in my bedroom. The clock read 8pm, but I had no idea if it was the same day or not. When Muriel's tornado had come for me, Jay had been waiting downstairs. He'd insisted I get some rest and it had been late afternoon. Ava smoothed her hair back into place from the windstorm. "Is it bad that I miss Evan already?"

"Me too," Cal piped in.

"Come on," I said, ignoring them. "We need to find Mom."

The house was so quiet that I didn't want to yell.

"Jay? Mom?" I whispered as we walked down the hallway toward the stairs. No answer.

"Mom?" I called in a louder voice.

"Bree? Is that you?" Mom's voice was shrill. Footsteps pounded and the door to her bedroom flew open. She looked a wreck. "Where have you been? Jay said you had to leave but he didn't know when you'd be back. How could you take off at a time like—oh my Lord!" She noticed Cal behind me. "Cal!"

She swept him up and pulled him to her while she cried into his hair. "My Cal. Thank the stars you're okay. My sweet, sweet boy." She pulled back to look at him. "Are you okay? What happened to you?"

Cal kept his arms tightly around Mom's neck. "I'm fine, Mom. I swear. I'm sorry you were so scared."

"Is Jay still here?" I asked.

Mom blinked. "No, he told me to call him as soon as you got back."

I didn't know how to ask the next question without sounding totally crazy. "But when was that, Mom? When did he leave?"

Concern and panic crossed her face. "Yesterday afternoon, Bree. Adrian called when you missed practice yesterday, but when I told him what happened to Cal, he said to send you his love."

"Wow, that doesn't sound like Adrian at all," Ava remarked.

Mom looked at Ava like she'd just noticed her. "And you. You missed practice too, and your mom called me and is worried sick. What is going on? Someone better tell me right now."

Ava and Cal both looked to me. I took a deep breath and sighed. Here went nothing. "Okay, Mom, but I think we should all sit down first."

I spoke for a while, with Ava and Cal filling in other bits and pieces. Cal mostly talked about his new brother Evan and how cool Liralelle was. Mom's face was like a stone mask as Ava babbled on about trolls, dwarves, and witches.

"Are you okay, Mom?" I asked. "I know it's a lot to digest."

"I don't know what to think," Mom said. "You have to give me time. But I need to tell the police you're both safe. They certainly won't believe your story, so I'll come up with something else." She stood up, still looking dazed. "Does Jay know about this Liralelle place?"

"Yeah, he's been there too," I said sheepishly.

"Everybody's been there apparently," she said in a tired voice. "Maybe someone will take me there to see it for myself."

"I will!" said Cal.

"Another day though," I said. "I need a little break."

Mom called the police, Ava called her mom to tell her she was fine and on her way home, and I called Jay.

He answered on the first ring. "Where are you? Are you okay? I've been worried sick."

"I'm home. Cal and Ava are with me. Everyone's fine."

Jay sighed in relief. "Thank god. I bet you have quite a story for me."

"I do. I'd rather tell you in person though, after I shower and sleep."

There was silence for a minute. "Okay, but no disappearing in the meantime."

I smiled. "Don't worry. I'm here for the long run. Jay?"

"Yeah?"

"It's good to hear your voice. I know it's only been a day here but I, uh, missed you."

I could hear his smile through the phone. "I missed you too."

MUSIC REVERBERATED through the theater and I could just make out Mom and Cal in the front row. I tried not to smile as Cal waved enthusiastically from his seat. The orchestra was below the stage but it was comforting knowing that Jay was there. During my last few weeks of rehearsals, Jay had dropped by the studio to watch. Adrian tried to shoo him away at first but relented and let him view practices through the observation window. We knew the performance was being filmed live, and after watching me practice, Jay told me that the recording should be all the audition I'd need to get into Juilliard. I hoped so. Especially if Jay would be there too.

Ava stayed with our family the past few weeks, while her mom got some help for her drinking. Her dad was basically living with his new girlfriend by this point. She was handling it pretty well all things considered. Rae came over one day and we had some good girl talks but we didn't tell her about Liralelle—I was worried she'd tell her mom who'd have us committed or something.

The spotlight centered on me and I danced and twirled just like I'd rehearsed for hours and hours. There were no trolls waiting when

I completed the rotations of my pirouettes and I lost myself in the flow of the performance. Ava and I exchanged smiles as she took the stage as the Canary Fairy. During the final curtain call, the audience rose to its feet, with no one yelling louder than Cal. The entire night felt magical.

Ava and I walked out to the lobby together and Jay waited near my mom and Cal with a bouquet of roses in his hands.

I smiled. "Are those for me?"

"Of course," he handed them to me. "It was between flowers and a zipper so I went with these."

"Huh?" Ava asked, and I laughed. Just then Ava's mom walked up.

"Ava?" she asked tentatively. "You were wonderful. Can I take you to a late dinner?"

Ava's face darkened but she nodded. "See you guys later."

I hugged Ava tightly. "You were fabulous, A. I'm so proud of you."

"Back atcha, B. Talk to you soon." Ava went to her mother, who put an awkward arm around her.

Cal hugged my waist. "I don't even like ballet that much, but you were awesome, Bree."

"You were great, sweetie," Mom said. "I just know you'll get into Juilliard."

When I showed Mom the sacks of gold I had stashed, she'd broken down and cried. That's when I think she really believed the crazy story we'd told her. She opted to keep working because she said she loved helping others, but said she'd cut back on her hours and would take time off more often.

"If it's okay with you, Mrs. McKenna," Jay started, "I'd like to take your daughter out to celebrate tonight. Like on a real date."

I nodded. "Not that Liralelle wasn't exciting and all that, but I'm ready for something more laid back, like pizza and a movie."

Mom sighed. "I guess it's okay. But no parallel-universe traveling and be home by 11pm Earth time please."

Jay saluted her. "Yes, ma'am. Got it."

"Thanks, Mom," I said. "See you in a few hours."

I CREPT into the house a few minutes before 11pm with a goofy smile plastered across my face. No way was I going to be home late and ruin my chances of more dates with Jay. We had the best time laughing and eating pizza. Not to mention the goodnight kiss he'd given me when he dropped me off at my house. It seemed crazy to think that we could both get into Juilliard and spend even more time together, but maybe fairytales weren't just for Liralelle.

Mom was sound asleep on the couch with the lamp still on. I turned off the light and kissed her cheek before covering her with a blanket. The house was quiet as I tiptoed up the stairs to my room.

"Bree!" Cal whispered loudly when I passed by his door.

"Cal, it's late. You're supposed to be asleep." I walked to his bed to kiss him goodnight.

He clicked on his reading light. "But I can't sleep. I've been trying for hours. Could you please read me just one story? Pretty please?"

I sighed. "Fine. Just one and then you have to promise to sleep in tomorrow. Mom doesn't work so we can all relax."

Cal reached over to the bookshelf next to his bed and pulled out the fairytale tome. "I promise."

I groaned. "Does it have to be that book?"

He flipped it open. "Yep. It's the best one there is. Let's see ..." His fingers flew down the index of fairytales and stopped on the last one. "That's weird."

"What? Let me see." I grabbed the book and looked where his finger had stopped. It was a fairytale I'd never heard of and certainly hadn't been there last time I'd read to Cal. It was called *The Witch and the Ballerina.*

"It's about you, isn't it?" Cal asked excitedly.

I turned to the page number listed in the book. The picture at the top of the story featured a ballerina in pointe shoes kicking a witch. Cal snuggled into me. "This is going to be the best one yet, I know it."

I smiled, put my arm around him, and began reading.

EPILOGUE

It was dark and damp. The air was colder down here; each tiny sliver of light immediately swallowed up by the blackness. Every movement caused excruciating pain and she wondered if she still had full use of all her limbs. Maybe her neck had been broken and she'd never be able to walk again or use her arms. She lay on the cot with her eyes closed and willed her gnarled hand to move.

Her fingers were balled into a fist and she strained with all her might. For a long moment, nothing happened. Then one of her fingers spasmed and moved an inch. She tried again. Finally, after what seemed like hours, all of her fingers uncurled and she stretched her hand out toward the wall. Her fingers brushed against it and the condensation from the stones was cool against her skin.

Gertrude opened her eyes and smiled.

ACKNOWLEDGMENTS

As the mother of a dancer, I've sat for hours watching ballet rehearsals, countless performances, dance conventions, and competitions. I think many people don't realize the amount of hard work, sweat, and tears that go into dance. On top of managing schoolwork and assignments, these young women and men are often in their studios well over 15 hours per week. This novel is an homage to all the dancers out there creating art and beauty in the world. Thank you!

A huge thank you to the Awesomesauce ARC Army who helped with the beta reading of this book, and a special shout out to Kyra who helped with a character name. You are all the best and I'm so happy to have you in my tribe.

To my writing partners in crime: Becky Taylor, Aimee Henley, and Shawn McGuire. I don't know what I'd do without you awesome ladies and your endless encouragement and inspiration.

A huge thank you to Wendy Terrien for reading an early version of this book and giving awesomely helpful feedback.

To the Bookclub Babes: I love you all and can't believe we've been talking books for 15+ years now!

To my family near and far, you are the best and thank you so much for your support!

Finally, a huge thank you to all the readers of the world. Writing for amazing readers is what makes it all worthwhile. I hope that even when the world becomes dark at times, you can find solace, and some hope, through reading. Escaping to another world, even for a short time, can provide respite and relaxation. Thank you for sharing this journey with me!

Make sure to sign up for my newsletter for upcoming releases, free short stories, giveaways and fun writing anecdotes at kristihelvig.com! You get a free short story immediately by signing up here.

PREVIEW OF THE WING COLLECTOR

DEAD THINGS

Epping Forest, England

September 8, 6:04 a.m.

I wait for her behind a large oak tree. Cool mist dampens the morning air, yet I feel no chill. I'm too focused. I know how it will unfold; the girl's initial confusion will give way to anger, then fear. Despite what I am about to do, I don't want her scared.

I want her dead.

Killing her is necessary in order to find the One. Streaks of gold penetrate the woods, and I watch the rising sun with impatience. The less light, the better. Light, tentative footsteps crunch the dead leaves underfoot.

The girl mumbles under her breath, "I don't know why we had to meet so early."

I take a slight step in her direction and a twig snaps.

She peers into the fog. "Matt?" she whispers. "Matt, is that you?"

I step out from behind the tree. "My deepest apologies, but Matt couldn't make it."

She starts to run when she sees the knife, and the crumpled note from her crush—as written by yours truly—slips from her hand. Her back turned to me only makes what I have to do easier.

I wipe the blood on a cloth that I'll later burn. One down, but many remain. I won't waver. I won't tire. I'll make the world a better place—one freak at a time.

Grab The Wing Collector on Amazon.

ABOUT THE AUTHOR

Kristi Helvig is a Ph.D. clinical psychologist turned sci-fi/fantasy author whose debut sci-fi novel, BURN OUT (Egmont USA/Lerner Publishing), was called "a scorching series opener not to be missed" by Kirkus Reviews. Her latest book, THE WING COLLECTOR (Dark Edge Publishing) is an urban fantasy involving a half-human/half-faerie teen who realizes her kind are being hunted when a pair of wings fetches big bucks in an online auction. Kristi muses about Star Trek, space monkeys, and other assorted topics on Facebook. Kristi resides in sunny Colorado with her hubby, two kiddos, and behaviorally-challenged dogs.

www.ingramcontent.com/pod-product-compliance
Lightning Source LLC
Chambersburg PA
CBHW020907180626
46816CB00007BA/2291